CHEMISTRY OF A KISS
A SWEET WATER HIGH ROMANCE

KIMBERLY KREY

Candle
House
Publishing

CHEMISTRY OF A KISS: A Sweet YA Romance

Sweet Water High Series Book 5

❀ Created with Vellum

WELCOME

Welcome to the town of Sweet Water,
North Carolina!

1 Town. 1 School. 12 Sweet Romances.

Misunderstanding the Billionaire's Heir: A Sweet YA
Romance (Sweet Water High Book 1)
by Anne-Marie Meyer (Author)

Crushing on My Brothers' Best Friend (Sweet Water High
Book 2) by Julia Keanini (Author)

Kissing The Boy Next Door (Sweet Water High Book 3)
by Judy Corry (Author)

Flirting with the Bad Boy (Sweet Water High Book 4) by
Michelle Pennington (Author)

Chemistry of a Kiss: A Sweet YA Romance (Sweet Water High Book 5)
by Kimberly Krey (Author)

Don't miss the next book in the Sweet Water High Series:
Falling for My Nemesis
by Tia Souders

CHAPTER ONE

*O*ne blackboard, twenty-six names, thirteen couples. That summed up the proverbial Strike Two in my day.

Exactly six seconds ago I hurried into class and scrolled down the lines of loopy cursive writing until I came to mine: *Harper Tisdale.*

A long dash separated my name from the one beside it. The name of my new partner—the one I would spend a dozen hours with over the next two weeks: *Jett Bryant.*

Anger, stress, tension, panic—all of it manifested itself in an annoying rash of heat along the back of my shoulders where it would grow and swell and force its way into other extremities. The mere sight of Jett's name next to mine set the heat wave in motion. I blinked hard, opened my eyes once more, but it was still there.

I knew something was wrong with this day from the moment I caught Missy eating the last bowl of the only decent cereal in the house. My stomach growled as I stared at the chalkboard in paralyzed horror. I wanted to bolt out of the classroom, push my way through the double doors at the hall's end, and head straight to The Bread Basket for a gooey cinnamon roll with extra icing, but that would do nothing to fix my problem. I'd come back tomorrow to find that Jett was still my partner. Worse, I'd have missed a day of class, meaning I would have to lean on *him* for the details of what I'd missed.

Students shuffled past me as they entered the room. Levi and Ky gave each other high fives after spotting the board and took a seat at one of the double desks in back. Another look at the board said Lauren and Lucas were paired up. Maybe we could switch.

Carefully, so as not to make accidental eye contact, I glanced over my shoulder to see if Jett had made it to class yet. Maybe he was sick today. I felt slightly hideous for hoping this was the case, but the fact was—in my heart—I was downright praying he was hovered over a barf bowl.

My hope was crushed when I noticed a confident-looking Jett stride into the room. Jett Bryant was never hard to spot in a crowd. That tall, self-assured stature combined with dark hair, an olive complexion, and ridiculously brooding eyes made him stand out among every other student at Sweet Water High. It had done the same thing all throughout middle school and elementary too. Trouble was, he seemed to know it.

I watched him from across the room, admiration clashing with angst like a war that would never cease. His brow furrowed as he took in the disrupted seating arrangement. He glanced up at the board next. My heart stopped beating for three full seconds as I scrutinized his face.

His dark eyes narrowed as he searched for his name, then widened as they stopped at one spot. A tiny tug pulled at the sides of his lips, making the angry shoulder heat shift into something a little less...angry. He moved his gaze over the room then, stopping only once his eyes met mine. That hint of a smile grew, each corner of his full lips lifting into a pompous grin.

Holy Gorgeous.

I jerked my eyes off him and faced the front of the room. Why did guys that attractive have to know what kind of effect they had on us? Probably because dummies like me made it obvious by doing stupid things to feed their ego.

One freaking kiss. That's all it was. One stupid kindergarten kiss and the guy thinks I'm in love with him for life. He probably thought I arranged this whole thing. The little pigtailed girl who chased him down, tackled him to the ground, and planted a kiss to his lips is trying a new tactic—magically becoming his partner in first period.

The bell rang out its obnoxious buzz, and the students hurried into their seats. Everyone but me. It was now or never. One of us had to be man enough to act, and since Jett was obviously enjoying himself too much to request a partner change, I'd woman-up and do it myself.

Ms. Tolken wasn't exactly the warm and fuzzy type, but she wasn't horrible either. I reminded myself that I aced debate class because I was good at presenting a case. I could do this.

Chin lifted, shoulders high, I strode to the front of her desk.

Tolken sat hovered over some paperwork, leaving me with a view of the bun in her hair, which was surprisingly big for the size of her head. She'd probably just broken out of her twenties but for some unknown reason she dressed like an eighty-year-old.

"Sorry to bother you, Ms. Tolken," I said in my sweet-but-assertive voice. The voice I used for Dorothy when approaching the Oz in Sweet Water's community production two summers ago.

"What is it?" the woman grumbled without looking up.

"I see that we have new partner assignments, and I wondered if it would be possible to make a slight change in mine."

The chatter behind me died down, allowing me to hear the actual seconds ticking by on the ancient clock by the window.

I glanced at the time, then back to her.

Had she heard me? Should I try again?

Perhaps if I leaned my hand beside her papers...I tried that, hoping it might remind Ms. Tolken that I was, in fact, waiting for an answer to my question. The shoulder heat climbed up the back of my neck.

The chatter picked up once more. Conversations about hangnails and ball practice and the Sadie Hawkins dance.

"Excuse me," I said, trying again. "I'm not sure if you heard me—"

"Who's your partner?" she snapped.

A glimmer of hope. "Jett Bryant," I whispered.

The woman lifted her chin at last, squinting at me through dark, thick frames. I doubted they were even prescription. Anything to make herself look less appealing... "The *pastor's* son?" The incredulous tone coating her words didn't escape me.

I shrugged, not sure why that mattered.

"You have a problem...with the pastor's son."

What, that suddenly made him perfect? "He's not as innocent as you think." I glanced over my shoulder, hoping no one had overheard, and kept it at a whisper. "We have some...bad blood," I explained.

Ms. Tolken held my gaze. "This is a class about relationships. Re-*lation*-ships!" she barked a second time, only louder now. "I suggest you use the skills you've learned in class thus far to become friends with Mr. Bryant." Suddenly, she pushed away from the desk, shot to her feet, and looked over the classroom like she was about to address them.

I hurried away from her toward the closest aisle, wondering if I could squeeze out the open window crack before she spoke up.

"Anyone else want to *try* asking for a partner change?" she asked.

My neck went fire-hot as I forced my eyes to the scuffed up floor. Thank heavens Jett had taken a seat at the back of the room. If he hadn't, I might have marched right out of the door and into the hall and bolted for that cinnamon roll after all.

Instead, I circled the desk, pulled the chair out, and sank into it with an inward groan.

"You didn't want to partner with my man Jett?" Ky asked.

Levi leaned around Ky and grinned. "Yeah, what's up with that?"

Cool, Harper. Play it cool. I pulled an innocent-looking face. "Where'd you guys get that idea?" I put some extra snark on the comment for their benefit and felt a grin coming on as the duo chuckled and shook their heads.

"I'm great with having Jett as my partner," I assured.

A heavenly, spicy scent wafted from Jett's side of the desk, reminding me of how close he was. I tucked my elbow against my ribcage to keep from touching him.

Focus, Harper. Do not let this affect your grade.

Ms. Tolken snatched a nub of chalk off the tray and shuffled over to the blank side of the blackboard. Why the woman refused to use a whiteboard like the rest of civilization was beyond me. "We're going to discuss a few popular relationship claims, and I'd like to know what you guys think of each." She stepped back to reveal what she'd just written: *You cannot make someone change.*

The woman dropped the chalk nub back onto the tray and dusted her hands on her pants. I worked to pull my eyes off the handprints, white against the brown polyester, as she addressed the class. "Do you agree or disagree, and why?"

"Disagree," I hollered. I knew this was a hot topic and that some would argue, but I had my reasons for feeling the way I did.

6

CHEMISTRY OF A KISS

"Harper." Ms. Tolken pointed a finger at me. "Stand up and tell us why. Why do you disagree?"

I pictured my boyfriend TJ. He had a bad-boy image, and in some ways he'd earned it. But I had fixed about a million things in my life so far and I was determined to fix TJ too. In fact, I was already making a difference. "I disagree full heartedly because people change all the time. My grandfather was an alcoholic for years, but eventually, he changed and it was all because of my grandma."

Ms. Tolken's gaze narrowed behind her thick rims, then darted over to Jett. "Do you agree with your partner, Mr. Bryant?"

My eyes widened as Jett stood to his feet. He folded his arms, causing the sleeve of his tee shirt to brush against my skin and that yummy, yummy scent of his to assault my senses. I shuffled away from him so we no longer touched.

"No, I do not," Jett said.

Big surprise.

"In fact," he continued, "I full heartedly *agree* with the statement on the board, Ms. Tolken. Sure, people change all the time. But they do it by setting their own mind to it, not because someone *made* them change."

I shook my head. "My grandfather said he got sober for my grandma and his kids."

"Yeah, but he had to do it on his own. Your grandma couldn't have *made* him do it."

Ms. Tolken put her hands up to stay us. "Thank you, thank you for your opinions. You two can sit down."

"I know the guy you're going out with," Jett mumbled once we took a seat.

I felt my eyes double in size. I could hardly believe he'd even dared bring him up. "Know him personally or just know *about* him?"

Ms. Tolken was already writing another statement on the board, not that my irritated eyes could even focus.

Jett came in closer, speaking just over my shoulder. "Both. And if you think you can turn him into some sort of Prince Charming, you're in for a rude awakening."

That got the heat going in my shoulders again. I turned in my seat to face him, ready to let loose, but was surprised by the expression on his face. It wasn't the challenging sort of sneer I expected to see. He looked...concerned.

I pulled in a breath, lips parted, suddenly forgetting what I wanted to say. Jett always did have the perfect-looking face. Aside from his amazing tan skin, he had a chiseled jawline most guys would kill for. And those eyes. Deep brown with swirls of gold. They were like secret weapons or something. I scrambled for what I'd planned to say.

"You have no right to judge TJ," I said. "In fact, didn't you hear your dad in service last week? He said there's only *one* Righteous Judge, and you and I both know that's not you." That was the ticket—bring Pastor Bryant into it.

"I'm not judging," Jett said with a shrug. "I just hate to see you waste your time on him, that's all."

Why did *he* care who I spent my time with? We'd barely said two words to each other since the eighth grade. A million weak rebuttals shot to my mind at once, but I bit all of them back and forced myself to read the next statement on the board.

Romantic chemistry is a real thing.

I contemplated that for a moment, not sure how I'd answer. It didn't strike a chord in me like the other one.

"I'd have to say *yes* to that one," Jett mumbled under his breath. He moved even closer, allowing his elbow to graze my bare arm. "What do *you* think?"

A zip of tingles rushed through me as I set my gaze back on him. I inched my arm away again because his touch was making my brain go soft. "No," I said in a whisper.

A half grin pulled at one side of his lips. Oh, man, I'd forgotten about that dimple. "No, what?" he challenged.

I needed to get serious about my position here, even if I'd only said no for argument's sake. "Well," I started, careful not to raise my voice. "I do not think romantic chemistry is a real thing because it suggests that people who don't even *like* each other could be attracted to one another." Why did it suddenly feel like I was describing the very phenomenon that was taking place in that moment?

I kept up with my argument. "And since I think that's impossible, I have to assume that this so-called *chemistry* people are experiencing is based on respect and love and...you know, things that matter."

"So does that mean you loved and respected me back in kindergarten when you—"

"Shhh," I scolded, not wanting him to say it aloud, even

if we were just whispering amongst ourselves. Geez, would he ever let go of that one? "I was curious when we were in kindergarten and you happened to be the slowest boy on the playground, which is the only reason I was able to catch you." *Lie.*

"And kiss me," he said.

Just hearing the words *kiss me* come from those lips while he was so close and yummy-smelling set me off balance in a major way. *Come on, Harper. Snap out of it.*

I pulled in a sharp breath and shifted in my seat. "You know, I'm starting to think that moment on the playground was the highlight of your life. And if it is, I feel sorry for you."

A laugh sounded from deep in his throat. "Maybe it was." His expression turned cryptic. "And we almost had a second chance at it. Until you chickened out."

My skin came alive with all sorts of conflicting tingles. He remembered that night too. The party at Connor's place. The one celebrating the end of middle school and the start of new adventures at Sweet Water High. Jett had made a fool of me in front of everyone, so I'd given it right back to him and basically hated him ever since. The thing was, his words seemed to be laced with regret.

At once, I pictured another offense: his ex-girlfriend, Tasha, smearing bright red lipstick over her pouty lips in the locker room a few months back. *"I heard you used to chase my boyfriend down and kiss him on the playground,"* she accused.

I hadn't given her a response, only finished tying my

shoes so I could get away from one of Sweet Water High's top MG's (code for mean girls).

"He says you still have a crush on him even now," she'd added. A cluster of her cronies laughed in the corner, whispering over high-pitched giggles.

My mom had always taught me that adamant denials made the accused appear guilty—the whole protesting too much sort of thing. And as much as I'd wanted to protest, as much as I'd wanted to say something like *in his dreams* or *your boyfriend is delusional,* I hadn't said a thing. Only snatched my gym bag off the ground, hiked it over my shoulder, and hurried into the hall.

Needless to say, Tasha had gotten the info from Jett, which reminded me of why I wasn't exactly a fan of his. A reminder I sort of needed with all the feels of attraction simmering through my body.

I managed to keep quiet the remainder of class, mainly because my mind was stuck trying to figure out how I would deal with being Jett's partner. I hated that I was attracted to him, and I didn't know what to do about all the tingles that zipped through me at his touch and his scent and even the low, raspy sound of his voice.

"Is it true that most of the rings you wear are from the plays you've been in?" Jett traced over the ring I wore on my pinky finger, causing a fresh bolt of electricity to course through me.

I couldn't help but wonder who he'd heard that from. Had he been talking about me? Asking about me, maybe? With just three minutes left of class, I dropped my gaze to look at the other rings I wore today. Three on my right hand and two on my left, each sterling silver. "Yeah," I answered. "A lot of them are. My granddad buys them for me. The tiny cat ears on this one is for…well you probably don't remember, but when I was in *The Aristocats* back in the third grade."

"I remember," he said. "And this one's for when you were Ariel?" He tapped the tiny mermaid on my pointer finger.

"Yes," I said, secretly loving how he remembered.

Jett grinned. "You were cute in that long, red wig."

My cheeks flushed with heat. "Thanks."

"Of course," he said under his breath, "I prefer brunettes."

I stiffened for a blink, liking the fact that I fit into that category.

"*And* green eyes," he added. Another feature that described me. He was probably just messing with me now. Next he'd say he liked theater girls who wore lots of rings.

"Here's the topic for you two," Ms. Tolken said as she shuffled up to our desk. She slid a bright red envelope onto the desktop and hurried over to Ky and Levi's next, sliding a pale green one before the pair. I glanced about to see the others in the classroom. Maddie's envelope was pale yellow. Another, deep blue. What was with the color-coding?

I looked back down at the envelope resting between Jett and me, feeling the heat of his gaze on my face. I glanced up to meet his eye.

Jett unleashed that grin of his. "Who's going to open

it?" He said it like it was a dare. Just ask Fiona Tisdale, my very intelligent mother, how well dares work on me.

I snatched the envelope, flipped open the unsealed flap, and pried it open with hurried fingers. There, tucked into the small space, bright white against the red, laid a slip of paper. Black ink spelled out our topic, the one we were meant to research—together—for the next two weeks.

Anticipation stirred wildly in my chest. My heart thumped out a few extra beats as I lifted my chin to locate Ms. Tolken. Her eyes were set right on me, and something in the sparkle behind those massive frames said she'd given us the topic on purpose.

"So?" Jett urged. "What does it say? What's our topic?"

I looked up to Jett, trying very hard not to focus on those big, kissable lips, and cleared my throat. "It's the Chemistry of a Kiss."

CHAPTER TWO

I do not want to kiss Jett Bryant. I do not want to kiss Jett Bryant. I have a boyfriend and he's the only guy I want.

It occurred to me as I waited for TJ to pull up to the curb in his dad's Chevy that I was chanting in my head. Who cared? It was all true. TJ was an amazing boyfriend who was taking time out of his day to come and get me from school so we could hang out.

A bright yellow school bus let out a loud whoosh as it came to a stop nearby. The doors hissed open, and a long line of students began filing in. Further down, students flooded the parking lot like insects in an ant farm, busily hurrying to get to the next place.

The chemistry of a kiss. What in the world kind of topic was that? And why did it keep triggering thoughts of that party back in middle school? Of the moment I decided *not* to kiss Jett Bryant. A decision that was either the best or the worst I'd ever made. It all depended on my mood.

I squinted against the sun, glad it had made an appearance today, and sighed. November in Sweet Water was chilly. Good thing I'd brought my jacket. I tightened it around me and folded my arms against the breeze. It was then I heard a loud, growling noise coming from the other side of the lot. I turned, a bit of dread sparking as I laid eyes on the sight. TJ, dressed in black from head to toe, straddled a massive motorcycle, his blondish brown hair tossing in the wind.

Was he kidding? I hated bikes. Hate hate hate.

"Tell me that is *not* your boyfriend."

I stiffened at the sound of Jett's voice. Talk about bad timing. Never once had TJ shown up on some sputtering death machine with black smoke pluming from the tailpipe.

TJ veered toward us, but he hadn't slowed down enough. My eyes widened in horror as the bike sped toward the curb just inches from my feet. The shortest distance between two points was a straight line, and if I didn't move out of the way in point five seconds, I'd become sidewalk kill in front of Jett and the awkward, gawking freshmen on the bus.

The thought came to me faster than my feet could move, but suddenly that didn't matter because a pair of strong arms hoisted me right off the ground and yanked me out of the way.

I felt myself teeter as my rescuer caught his footing, the masculine, spicy scent of him confirming just who it was. A large hand cradled my hip as I steadied my feet and spun to face him. He hadn't exactly let go of me yet, so that put us face to face and hands (mine) to chest (his). At least it hadn't gone the other way around; the freshmen would have really had something to talk about then.

"Are you okay?" he breathed, concern etched on his handsome face.

"Me?" I squeaked. *Whoa.* That was one muscled chest. I forced my palms away from the wonderfully warm contours and nodded. "I'm...yes. Thank you." I stepped back and spun to see what had happened to TJ.

Beyond a crowd of mumbling spectators, I caught sight of a spinning tire. The bike had made it up the stairs, a small flight of half a dozen, and was sputtering on its side, spewing plumes of black smoke.

"That was wicked," TJ bellowed as he leaned down to pick up the bike.

"You know, you were right," Jett said.

I tore my eyes off the sight to glance over at Jett, not fully able to wipe the annoyed sneer off my face. TJ had nearly killed me and all he was doing was soaking up the glory of a bunch of high school kids.

Jett tipped his head to one side. "He seems...*nice.* A real Prince Charming, right there."

Angry heat climbed right up my back and into my neck. I glared at Jett, feeling torn after he'd just come to my rescue moments ago. What kind of game was he playing? I shook my head, set my eyes back on the crowd surrounding TJ, and tugged the phone from my pocket.

Forget about TJ and Jett. I needed to get out of there, and fast.

---

*T*he oven glowed bright as I pried open the door. A casserole dish with only heaven knew what rested in Mom's favorite blue dish. I wished I could say that the aroma made my mouth water, but it came closer to triggering my gag reflex than anything else.

My bottom lip curled. My stomach heaved. Why Mom had to experiment with every creation under the sun was beyond me. No, not *every* creation. Only the fifty competitors for nastiest healthy food meals. I was positive there were decent options out there too; Mom just didn't know how to choose them.

"Is it almost ready?"

"Yeah," came TJ next. "It smells good, and I'm starving."

I shrugged, amazed that either of them wanted to taste the source of the smell in the air. Who walked into a sewer, sucked in a long breath, and asked when dinner was?

"Sure," I said, snatching the potholders off the counter. Heat from the open door flooded over my face and arms as I lifted the dish out and onto the stovetop. "Come and get it."

Missy galloped over while spanking her own butt and neighed. Perhaps if I pretended this was horse food I'd enjoy it too. I handed over her favorite plate, the one with cats in a basket, then retrieved the matching cup as well.

17

Unsure whether spoons or forks were called for, I pulled two of each out of the drawer and slid them onto the counter.

"Aren't you going to eat?" TJ asked as he piled the grainy goo onto his plate.

"Nope."

"What time is Mom going to be home?" Missy asked in a singsong voice.

I glanced at the clock on the microwave. "Probably not for a few more hours. The house she's showing is far away."

"Does that mean we can watch TV on the trays while we eat?"

"Sure," I said, heading over to the pantry. "TJ will turn it on for you, okay?" The door made that haunted house-sounding creak when I swung it open, which felt oddly appropriate considering the sight beyond was sure to be scary. Dry grain in boxes and bins. Tubs of powder and supplements and freeze-dried everything from peas to prunes. I tipped my head back and groaned. "For the love," I cried. "Why can't we have normal food in this house?" I stepped further into the depths when a gold wrapper caught my eye.

Could it be? It was. I snatched the small bar from its hidden place behind the organic prune juice (what, was Mom dipping into Ms. Tolken's pantry now?) and grinned. A protein bar with real peanut butter in it. *This* was the reason I actually liked school lunch. I was deprived. Fiona Tisdale might insist on buying all things natural, but the fact was, there was nothing natural about eating the stuff stacked on the shelves.

I sank onto the couch and watched wrestling with TJ and Missy. I told myself, as Missy yelled at the big screen on demand, smiling over at TJ for approval, that he would make a good dad one day. He would. He was cute with Missy. And the incident with the bike had been a freak accident. What, did I expect him to be perfect? How fair was that?

TJ patted the couch cushion beside him and lifted his brows. He tipped his head toward Missy. I followed the motion to see that she'd fallen asleep. *Oh,* and TJ wanted to get close. So did I. I mean, it hadn't occurred to me or anything. I hadn't been like, *when is this kid going to fall asleep so we can be alone?* But I was still glad.

I slid over to close the gap and rested my head onto his chest. I sighed. This was nice. I was happy with TJ. He was a good guy. Who probably very much wanted to apologize for his rude behavior at the school. Maybe he was working up to that in his mind.

The fact was, he didn't follow me straight home after the incident. In fact, I'd spent forty angry minutes crossing off Mom's to-do list while waiting for him to show up and apologize exactly in that order. He'd accomplished the showing up part, but had yet to get to the apology. I figured now that he'd finished off half of Mom's mystery casserole, bless him, he was ready.

"That was a little crazy today in the parking lot," I said, steering him in the right direction.

He ran a hand through his shaggy blonde hair and

grinned. "Yeah, that was wicked. I don't really know how to drive it too well yet, but if I'm going to buy it, I better figure it out quick."

The words were a set of screeching brakes in my head. *Buy it?* Had he forgotten his goals? Had he forgotten the black pluming smoke and sputtering engine?

TJ wrapped an arm around me and pulled me against him. And suddenly he was leaning in for a kiss. Eyes closed. Lips puckered.

Not so fast. "Wait," I said. "Did you…" I stopped there to rephrase the question. "You decided last week that you wanted to save up and go to school. Remember?"

TJ pulled back and looked at me through half closed lids. "Yeah, babe, but then I talked with the guys today and they're getting real serious about Grunge Town. They want to try and take it on the road. Record an album maybe." He lifted a brow. "Isn't that awesome?"

I smiled, wondering why we always ended up in this same spot. And then I remembered something. "You were with the band today? I thought you had work."

He gave me the exact same look I've caught Missy giving Mom, those please-don't-be-mad-at-me eyes.

"*What?*" I said, relating with my poor mother more than ever before.

"I called in sick. Jessie was stoked about this new riff he came up with last night at like, two in the morning. He texted the band with a 911 and was like, '*we seriously have to jam today.*'"

I huffed out an exaggerated sigh. There weren't a

whole lot of items on the list I'd made with him. In fact, I had it memorized by heart.

Save money.

Ask for raise and take extra shifts.

Pick college or training and set a start goal.

I could feel myself wadding up the proverbial towel. I wanted to bolt out of the house, run to the nearest cliff, and chuck it into the pit of forgotten hopes and failed dreams. I didn't want to do this anymore. Yes, I was attracted to TJ and the whole bad-boy thing he had going on. He was so very opposite me, and I think that's what drew me to him the most.

The trouble was, I was *more* attracted to the guy he *would* become once he was done with this phase. Sure, I wanted a guy with an edge, but I didn't want him to be a total bum. The debate I had with Jett earlier ran through my mind. He'd insisted I couldn't change TJ, and I was actually starting to wonder if he was right. Immediately I envisioned the assignment in that red envelope. The chemistry of a kiss.

In our three and a half weeks of dating, TJ and I hadn't had what I'd call an amazing kiss. He'd started giving me goodbye kisses after our second date—date being a loose term since TJ wasn't exactly the let's-go-to-dinner-and-the-movies type of guy. He was more of the let's-hang-out-and-watch-movies type. Or the hey-wanna-come-watch-us-jam-in-Jessie's-garage type.

I didn't mind at first. In fact, it was all part of the excitement of dating a rebel. But already, the novelty was wearing thin. *Stop,* I told myself. I needed to stop giving myself a way out. It might not be easy, but I needed to stick this out and help TJ become his best self. It'd be worth it.

TJ leaned in and kissed my cheek. A soft, lingering kiss. It felt nice, and I couldn't help but wonder what it might feel like to have that exact soft kiss on my lips. We'd only shared one long, close-to-make-out type of kiss, and it wasn't all that great. TJ had come into it with too much...enthusiasm. It was like he'd never watched the movies where characters actually worked up to kisses like that.

I wanted to see what it felt like when he really relaxed and let it happen naturally. Especially now since ideas of kissing Jett had crossed my mind. I needed to replace those evil visions with a mind-blowing kiss from TJ, meaning the lecture about his goals would have to wait until we rekindled a little love.

I grinned, gave him a little encouragement by planting a playful peck to his lips in return, and suddenly TJ moved in with a groan. His lips were desperate and demanding and...and gross. It felt like I was kissing that nasty casserole Mom made.

Instinctively, I moved my hands to his chest and pushed, breaking the seal of our lips. I gasped there for a quiet second while TJ stared at me with his lips still parted.

That was bad. That was really, really bad. How many things would I have to fix in this relationship before we'd be sailing smooth?

"Sorry," I breathed. I looked over to where Missy had fallen asleep.

"Don't worry about it," TJ mumbled.

Oh, TJ thought I'd stopped things because of Missy.

A grin spread over his mouth. "She's out like a light." He wrapped a hand around the back of my neck, ready to draw me in for more, when a voice spoke up.

"What's going on in here?"

Ah, thank heavens. It was Mom.

"Nothing," I said and scooted myself back onto the other cushion.

"Oh yes there is," Missy chimed. "They were *kissing!* I saw them."

CHAPTER THREE

*T*he sky was a giant sheet of clouds as I trudged down the steps toward Bailey's car. It matched my mood to a tee. Thank heavens she and Summer had been able to pick me up again; we were down to one car until Mom renewed the registration on her Nissan, which meant she had to take the Jetta to work again.

I pried open the door, climbed into the back seat, and closed the door behind me. "You're not going to believe what happened last night," I said while strapping my seatbelt on.

Summer spun in place, her blonde hair flying off her back and settling over the front of her shoulders. "What?"

Bailey caught my eye contact through the rearview. "Do tell."

"My mom said I'm not allowed to date *just* TJ. I have to date someone else in between."

"No way."

"You're kidding!"

"Nope."

Summer's face scrunched up. "Why?"

I didn't exactly want to get into that part. The truth was, it had taken me a while to get over the whole casserole kiss, but now that Mom was trying to set such ridiculous boundaries to keep me from getting "too serious" with TJ, I was more Team TJ than I'd ever been before. I really liked him. He'd been so cute with Missy. And when he'd kissed my cheeks all soft and feather-like, it had been amazing.

"Were you two making out?" Bailey asked in my silence.

I stared at the back of her head. She had her red hair pulled back today and twisted into a knot. "Not exactly," I mumbled. "But Missy made it sound like we were."

Summer gasped. "You were kissing in front of your little sister?"

"She was asleep," I said, irritated.

"So what are you going to do?" Bailey asked.

I tipped my head back dramatically and groaned. "I have no idea. I don't want to date anyone else." I was glad to realize that my words were still true. Sure, I might have gotten a little distracted by Jett and his incredible smell and eyes and brooding appeal, but I wasn't going to give up on TJ so soon.

Besides, what would that do really? Prove to Mr. Pompous that he'd been right on now *two* counts. One, that I couldn't, in fact, make TJ change. The second one would be more implied than anything, but if I broke things off now, right after Jett had swooped in like a dark, dangerous superhero and rescued me from TJ's bike, Jett was sure to flatter himself and assume I was interested in him. Which I one hundred percent was not. And no, I wasn't *protesting too much*, I was stating the facts.

"You're going to have to find someone else to date," Summer said.

"Someone safe," Bailey suggested, "like a guy who's already in the friend zone."

Summer grinned wide. "That's a good idea. You could like, be doing homework or something, but tell your mom you're going on a date."

I considered that. Not a bad idea actually. "Huh."

"Hey," Bailey blurted. "Jett!"

My face went hot. *"What?"*

"You two are partners now in Dating and Relationships class, right?"

"How'd *you* know that?"

Summer shrugged. "Caleb told us."

"Caleb isn't even in that class," I said.

"Yeah, but he's Jett's friend." Bailey pulled into a parking stall, shut off the engine, and spun around to look at me over her shoulder. "What are you getting so flustered about? You seem weird."

"I already *told* you what I'm upset about," I said, hating how she could read every detail of my face and voice and posture. We knew each other too well.

"You look really pretty today," Summer said in the quiet pause. "Did you do your eyes different?"

"Maybe a little." I thought back on the half-dozen

tutorials I'd watched about how to make my green eyes pop. Not because I was attracted to Mr. Brown eyes (how could I be, I didn't even like him) but because it seemed only fair to even out the playing field. I was dealing with a guy who had serious good looks on his side.

"Are you going to ask Jett?" Summer was already getting out of the car. Bailey was too. I released another groan.

"Can't I just sit in the car all day?" I pleaded.

Bailey opened the back door and leaned far over to face me, her red hair complimenting the pink in her cheeks. "I don't know what the deal is. You have a problem. We have a solution."

I looked down at the arm she offered before reaching out with a limp hand of my own. We were halfway through the parking lot when I spoke up once more. "I don't want to even see Jett right now."

"Well, I've got a solution for that too. There's an assembly today. You won't even go to your first period."

"We still have to go and let them take roll," I said, but Summer shook her head.

"Not today. They're skipping that."

I didn't have a clue why that tidbit made me feel even worse. "What would it even look like? If I *did* try and use Jett as my alternate dates?"

Bailey tipped her head to one side. "You'd just ask him to study with you a couple of times a week, which you'll have to do anyway, and maybe, I don't know, go to his place or the library or even to the Burger Bar. Make it look like a date."

"And it's not really wrong because you really *are* seeing a different guy in between each of your dates with TJ, which is what your mom wants," Summer said. Bless her, always keeping things on the up and up. If my sweet friend's personality was actually summer, like her name, I was something a little darker. Fall, I guess. Bailey was spring, because she was good at breathing new life into things. Guess that left cold and bitter Mr. Winter for Jett.

I grinned a little at that. It was probably a very good thing that I didn't have my class with Jett today. I needed more time to clear my mind and come up with a plan of attack. Or was it defense?

"Oh my gosh, there he is," Bailey said, smacking my arm with the back of her hand. "It's Jett."

My heart thundered like a team of wild horses were trotting through it. Jett was walking up the very steps TJ had crashed that dumb bike on yesterday.

Summer gave me a nudge. "Go ask him if he can study with you tonight."

My throat clenched up. "No, I don't want him to think I'm like, seriously trying to date him."

"Then tell him you need his help," Bailey said. "Just be honest about your situation. He won't mind."

"Yes, he will," Summer blurted. She hurried to come around and stop me from taking another step, her eyes wide and worried. "You can't tell him you're using him. That's just rude."

"I think it's rude if she *doesn't*," Bailey argued.

I looked past Summer to see Jett pull open the door

and walk through. Man, even from behind you could tell he was attractive.

"You know what?" I said. "It doesn't matter. I'll find another way."

Summer and Bailey looked at one another before setting their gaze back on me. "If you say so," Summer mumbled.

Bailey shrugged in that way she always did when she was annoyed with me. "Fine. Whatever."

I sighed, glad I'd been saved from *that* one. Call it pride or stubbornness or stubborn pride, but I did *not* want Jett to think I needed him for anything and I definitely couldn't have him flattering himself by thinking I was secretly interested in him.

I thought about how *not* interested in him I was during the entire assembly. And throughout my next few classes as well. *I'm not interested in Jett. The whole reason I'd even consider asking him to help me is so that I could keep on dating TJ. Sweet TJ who watched wrestling with Missy and made her smile and...* I stopped myself there. Positive things only. I'd focus on the positives and help him change the rest.

By the time lunch came around, I was still torn about whether or not I should ask Jett to help out. At least I had until tomorrow to decide.

"So what's the deal with the *spin the bottle* incident?" Summer piped as she stabbed a heap of lettuce onto her fork.

The cafeteria was alive with clanking chairs, sliding trays, and a million voices talking all at once. But at the sound of Summer's question, all of it vanished. "Who told you about that?" I scanned the line to see Bailey, foot tapping the floor while her thumb tapped her phone screen. "What did she tell you about it?"

Summer hadn't been at the eighth grade party like Bailey had, and the truth was, I didn't like discussing the incident.

"Oh, Bailey didn't tell me about it. Caleb did. But he wouldn't say exactly what happened either. Just that you were mad or something."

I rolled my eyes and wondered how fast I could spit it out before Bailey got back; I didn't want the topic to dwell all through lunch. "A long time ago when we were in kindergarten, I chased him down and kissed him."

"Aw, that's so cute!"

I nodded and leaned forward. "Yeah, well I thought he was cute, no big deal. But years later we were at a party playing spin the bottle and when it was my turn, it landed on him."

Summer squealed and leaned closer in return.

I didn't want to admit that I was glad about it, so I skipped that detail and went on. "So I looked at him for a minute, trying to see if I should go to him or if he was going to come to me, and suddenly he says, 'Come on over. This time, I won't even make you chase me.'" Heat gathered in my shoulders at the mere recollection.

"That's so darling!" Summer gushed.

I stared at her with a shocked face. "No, it was *rude*. Everyone at the whole party was like, 'Ooohhhh,' and 'aaahhhh,' and 'daaaaang!' It made me look like some dumb little puppy dog who'd been chasing after him all those years only to spin the bottle in some contrived way so it would land on him."

"Maybe you took it wrong."

"I didn't. You should have seen how smug he looked."

Summer popped a grape in her mouth and nodded thoughtfully. "So did you kiss then or not?"

This is where the love/hate situation warred in my head. More with myself than with him. What would have happened if we had just kissed that day? What if it would have been amazing? Something told me that it would have been, and that something made me hate the decision I made.

I sighed, not wanting to share this part after the way Summer responded to the rest, but I did it anyway. "I started walking toward him, and even though everyone else had clustered into groups so they could get a better view, Jett stayed right in one spot. That *really* ticked me off. It made it seem like I was just making the move on him all over again. And just as I got closer, this major smirk came over his face. Like this confident, I-knew-you-wanted-me sort of grin. And that was it for me."

"So what'd you do?"

"I stopped walking, looked him in the eye, and said, 'On second thought, I'm pretty sure that bottle was pointing somewhere else. Who was standing beside Jett?'"

Summer gasped and covered her mouth. "No, you didn't!"

"Yep. I did."

"And did someone speak up?"

"*Three* guys spoke up," I said proudly. "Wes and Caleb,

who really *had* been standing beside him, and this guy named James. He hadn't been standing by him at all, but just the fact that he wanted to kiss me enough to lie over it…that's what made me pick him." My face flushed with embarrassed heat. "I planted a pretty good kiss on him, too. Right in front of Jett. And that was it."

"Wow." Summer leaned an elbow onto the table and reached for her sandwich. She lifted it to her mouth, readied to take a bite, but paused for a blink. "I still don't think what he said was all that bad. You probably just took it wrong."

"Took *what* wrong?" Bailey pushed her tray onto the table and set her milk carton alongside.

I shook my head no at Summer before she could say anything. "Nothing." I looked down at the chicken sandwich on my plate, knowing I should be starving. This was not a good time to lose my appetite. It was, like, my only chance to eat normal food.

As I stared down at my tray, willing myself to at least shove in a few fries, I felt something shift at the table, like suddenly all eyes were on me. I lifted my chin to see that I was right. Summer, Maddie, and Bailey were all looking at me with wide eyes. Well, not exactly *at* me. It was more *behind* me. Even Lauren, who was walking toward us, tray in hand, had her eyes pasted on the same spot.

I spun to look over my shoulder, already knowing who I'd see. And there he was, those smoldering brown eyes fixed in my direction.

"Hey there." He eased into a grin before hunching down to my level. His hand brushed my knee, and suddenly the tingles were happening everywhere. It didn't help that he was wearing that same deliciously masculine cologne again. "I was thinking that maybe, since we weren't able to get started in class today, we could get together after school and see what this project is all about."

I stared at him while my brain tried to make something very clear to the rest of my oddly reacting body: *He's not asking you out, Harper.* This was all about our school assignment. An assignment that included spending time with our partners outside of class.

"That's probably a good idea," I said.

He grinned. "Right after school good for you?"

I nodded, but I should've been shaking my head instead. "Well, I have to watch my little sister after school, but maybe later tonight I could come out? Like at seven or so?" I suddenly felt like a swindler for not telling him about my ulterior motive. But then I remembered that I really did have to study with him either way. What difference did it make if I used it to appease my mom?

"Hey, everybody. Look this way and let me catch a picture of you guys." I glanced up to see Emmy, one of Sweet Water High's photographers, peeking around the giant lens of her camera. "Jett, scoot a little closer to Harper."

Jett surprised me by placing an arm around my back, cupping my shoulder, and bringing his cheek very close to mine. Did I mention he smelled amazing? My body responded with doses of heat and tingles and, most likely, two very pink cheeks as I put a grin on my face.

"Perfect!" Emmy hunched behind the lens once more. She wasn't exactly *Team Tasha* either. I had a hunch she was capturing a picture of me and Jett to spite Tasha and her band of mean girls. Bless her for that.

"Thanks, guys," Emmy piped before scanning the cafeteria once more.

Jett gave my shoulder a subtle squeeze, then shot to a stand and jutted his chin toward our table. "See you guys."

"Bye," they sang out in chorus.

"See *you* tonight," he said, pinning one last look at me before walking away.

I gulped, nodded, then scanned over the faces of the girls at my table. Flushed cheeks, fluttering lashes, and wide smiles. Jett definitely had an effect on the opposite sex.

Who cared? That didn't mean I had to let him have such an effect on me.

"Dang, he is *so* hot," one mumbled.

My heart suffered a small pang. Yes, Jett really was. And what if Summer was right? What if he wasn't so bad after all?

A knot of guilt spread through my gut. How was I ever going to help TJ change if I was this easily distracted? But then another thought seeped in, raising a more immediate question. Jett Bryant and I were researching the chemistry of a kiss. Together. Tonight. What in the world would that be like?

CHAPTER FOUR

I decided to study before going over to Jett's house for the night. Not about our project, but about methods I could use to stay focused on my goals. My main goal for the time being was to stay with TJ.

Some might think that was shallow or lame, but I didn't like quitters. I wasn't a quitter. I was a fixer. Just ask Mom and her list of things for me to do. I hovered over said list as the minutes counted down. In less than five minutes, Mom would be home and I'd be on my way.

I'd already borrowed the Jackson's ladder and replaced the light bulbs in the stairwell and the garage. *Check.* I'd fixed the issue Mom had with the remote in her bedroom. *Check.* I'd read with Missy, gave her the rest of the leftover casserole, and now there was just one thing left. Take out the trash.

The garage door opened, and Missy climbed off the

couch and began hopping in place on the floor. "Mom's home!"

"Yep," I said, a flare of nerves building up in my chest. I snatched my bag off the counter and looped it over my shoulder on the way out the door. "See you later, Missy Moo."

She grinned at me with her tiny teeth. "See you later, Harper Loo."

I was halfway down the first stair when I remembered the garbage. Quickly, I darted back inside and crossed the kitchen. I steadied the base with my foot and pulled the thing free. "Bye bye, sugar pie," I said this time.

"Bye bye, apple stink pie!"

I chuckled and pointed my finger at her. "Hey!"

Missy plopped back onto the couch and giggled wildly.

"What's so funny?" my mom asked as she stepped inside. Two reusable grocery bags hung from her grip.

"Please tell me you have some protein bars in there," I said. "I've been, like, living off apples and that scratchy bread for weeks."

"I've got a few in here," Mom said, "but I wish you'd give some of these new recipes more of a try."

That wasn't going to happen. "Alright, well I'm off to my date."

"With Pastor Bryant's son?" Mom asked.

"Yep." I didn't want to get into this. I'd texted her from school shortly after the plan was hatched and hoped she wouldn't ask a bunch of questions. She hadn't, but she might list them all off now.

"Well, I've always wondered why you didn't date him, Harper. That is one good-looking kid."

The garbage was growing heavier in my hand. "I'll be sure to tell Pastor Bryant and his wife you said so."

"Oh, honey, didn't you hear? They're separated."

My eyes went wide. "What? I thought his mom was just helping her mother in Atlanta."

Sadness always showed itself in my mom's eyes. The way they'd get heavy and slanted. She shook her head. "Yeah, I think it kind of started out that way. I'm sure they're keeping it under wraps until they know what's going to happen. I think that, for a pastor who wants to keep it all together, it'd be even harder to go through something like this."

I nodded as I considered that. "You're right. Well, I won't be out too late."

"Okay. And hopefully you can cheer Jett up. This can't be easy for him either."

No, it couldn't.

I lifted the lid off the garbage and hoisted the bag into the bin. It was dark out, the hours getting shorter now that we'd "fallen back" in time.

On the drive there, the black night seemed to creep into the car and sit with me. Jett's parents were separated. That was awful. It made me see him in a new light. A light where he wasn't just a pompous guy with incredible good looks and a swelling ego. He was a guy who...who was probably trying to keep his family together, the way I had done. Well, not successfully, but I had tried. And tried and tried. But really, what was I going to do? Rescue my parent's marriage at the meager age of ten?

But then his words came back to me. *I full heartedly agree with this statement. You cannot make somebody change.* I'd assumed he'd said that with Tasha in mind, seeing that he and his wild ex-girlfriend had recently broken up.

Sweet Water Chapel looked a little different to me as I passed it. Outdoor floodlights lit the place up from the outside, making the white, steepled structure stand out against the dark night. Pastor Bryant often said we were all broken in our own way; I just hadn't imagined that he'd been talking about himself and his wife as well.

I squinted as I pulled into Jett's cul-de-sac, noticing a man by the curb. As I neared, the headlights illuminating his tall, muscled build, I realized it was Jett, taking the trash out as well. He tossed a bag in, lowered the lid, then squinted against the light as he turned in my direction.

My heart skipped.

Quickly, I flicked off my lights, put it in park, and shut off the engine. I snatched my phone out of the cup holder and reached for my bag, when suddenly my interior light kicked on and a rush of cold air came from behind.

"Hi," Jett said. "Can I help you with that?"

Bag in hand, I glanced over my shoulder and lifted a brow. "With what?"

He tucked his fingers beneath the straps of my bag and took it from me. "This." I stared at him for a minute and tried to force myself to move.

Jett hoisted the strap over his shoulder and held his hand out for me to take. This was new. I stared at his offered palm, wondering if this was the kind of treatment Tasha got while they dated.

"Thank you," I said, and placed my hand in his. I couldn't help but revel in the feel of his strong hand around mine as I climbed out of the car. If you'd have asked me yesterday if I was a fan of chivalry I might have likely said no. But that was because I'd never experienced it before.

Jett closed my door for me while still holding onto my hand. The realization made me pull it away. I felt rude after doing it, so I played with my hair to make the action look necessary.

"It's a pretty night," Jett said.

Aside from the sight of the Sweet Water Chapel, I hadn't paid much attention. I looked up to see a stretch of wispy clouds circling the bright moon. The light from it reached all the way to the small town of Sweet Water, where it lit Jett's face up like a spotlight on a Greek god. "Yeah," I agreed.

Jett pulled a grin that triggered that million-dollar dimple.

I gulped. *Holy holy.* I was in trouble now.

He led me through the front room and into the kitchen where a dining table stood beneath a hanging light. "I figured we'd study in here," he mumbled. "Is that okay?"

I nodded, wondering what that delicious aroma was. I glanced over to see a pan on the counter. Corndogs and french fries were spread over the surface. *Normal food!* It looked and smelled so good.

"You hungry?"

I pulled my gaze off the pan since I was probably looking at it like a starving person. "No. Not really."

Jett seemed to study me for a blink. "I made too much. My mom, she's, uh, taking care of my grandma in Atlanta, and Ava and Ivy are gone for the night, so I'm just going to have to toss it all in the fridge."

I glanced at the food once more, and I swear the action made my stomach moan. It wasn't that my mom didn't feed me. Heck, she tried to feed us better than any mom in town. I just couldn't palate the disgusting taste of it all.

"Here." Jett moved into the kitchen and snatched a paper plate off the counter. Using a pair of tongs, he placed a corndog, some fries, and a few square-shaped things I didn't recognize onto the center. "Want ketchup? Mustard? Ranch?"

I nodded as my stomach growled.

Jett chuckled under his breath. I watched him retrieve the condiments from the fridge while my backpack hung off one muscular shoulder. The white shirt he wore was clearly an undershirt, the thin fabric revealing the muscled contours of his chest. A chest I'd had my hands on, actually. *Get it together, Harper. You're at the pastor's house, for crying out loud.*

"So where's your dad tonight?" I asked.

Jett's face scrunched up as he splatted mustard beside the ketchup blob. "Counseling," he said.

I lifted my brows, wondering if Jett was going to tell me about his parent's situation after all.

"He counsels couples from church, you know? As part of the job."

"Oh, yeah. That makes sense." I knew that what Jett said was true, but could it be that the counseling session Pastor Bryant was at was for him and his wife? One of those video chats, maybe. I wanted very badly for Jett to open up to me about it. I had no idea why. Except for that I'd been through it already. Watched the two most important people in my life tear apart in a world of angry words and bitter tears. Maybe I could help him.

"So do you plan to major in theater at UNCW?" he asked.

I shot him a how-did-you-know-I-was-going-there look, but he just grinned. "I helped Pastor Bri pick out cards and candy for all the students who got scholarships," he explained.

"Ah, that makes sense." Bri was the youth pastor at church. "And no. Theater's fun, but I never wanted to pursue it beyond high school. In fact, rather than try out for a lead this year, I told Mr. Meadows I just wanted to be in the ensemble."

I guessed since Jett knew so much about me I could admit to knowing a little about him in return. "I heard you're also going to UNCW. You got a basketball scholarship, right?"

He grinned. "Yep. I'll be playing for the Seahawks," he said.

I kind of liked how...*together* he was. Compared to TJ, especially. "Nice," I said, remembering the excitement when the university came to scout him out. "What will your major be?" I asked.

"Civil engineering," he answered.

My face scrunched up. "So you'll be doing what when you graduate, exactly?"

He chuckled. "Most likely I'll be designing or maintaining infrastructure projects like roads, tunnels, airports, bridges. That type of thing."

"Wow," I said, and I meant it. "That's cool."

"What are you majoring in?" he asked.

"Business. I figure that's broad enough I should have some good options."

"Why don't you go ahead and eat, and I'll see if I can pull up some info about this." He brought the plate over to me and slid it onto the oak table.

Warm light spilled over the floral design casing the paper plate. It wasn't as if he'd slaved over a five-course meal or anything, but he may as well have. As horrible as it might seem, this was the food I dreamt of. The stuff normal families ate when soccer practice and theater fell on the same night. Or when Mom shuffled in after a late day in the office.

"Thank you," I said before reaching for the square thing first. I stared at the sauces for a blink.

"That one goes in ranch."

"Oh," I said. "There's pizza in this one, right?"

He smiled wide. "Right."

"I had these at Bailey's house forever ago." I dipped it, took a bite, and groaned from the incredible flavor. "This is amazing," I said before dipping it again.

"Yeah," he said. "I love those things."

A sense of comfort fell over me, and suddenly, I felt very much at home. Jett cracked open a laptop and pulled up an article about the origins of the kiss. Sounded like a good place to start.

He read aloud while I worked on the food—dipping, eating, and nodding along. According to one article, the act of kissing dated all the way back to 1500 B.C. There was conflicting evidence as to how many cultures actually kissed—some said ninety percent of them; another said it was closer to fifty—but one thing was widely agreed: people liked doing it.

"It says here that they used to sign documents with an X and then give it a kiss, which still exists today, hence the use of X's and O's when we sign a letter."

"That's so cool," I said. "I wonder where the O's came from."

"That's a good question." He squinted back at the screen and continued.

I looked at him as he read aloud, imagining what it might be like to sit across from him twenty years from now, a few kids playing out in the backyard while he read me an article from the newspaper. Would he be wearing a white collared shirt, the top few buttons undone while his loosened tie hung just beneath? Or would it be more of a Sunday morning thing? Both of us lounging in our robes, mugs of coffee resting before us. Would he have a five o'clock shadow along that chiseled jaw of his?

I sighed. He just seemed so...solid. And for whatever reason, I appreciated that more than ever. I knew—by rumors of what happened at Carl Macky's kegger—that Jett had sown a few wild oats. With him being the pastor's son, it seemed everyone knew. But Jett had it together now. At least he seemed to.

The sight of my empty plate save the corndog stick sent a splash of embarrassment through me. I hopped up, walked into the kitchen, and found the trash bin under the sink. Worried that my hands now smelled like food, I washed up with a squirt of yummy-scented soap, something Cathy had bought for sure.

"So," Jett said. "That revealed a lot about the history of the kiss, but not so much about the chemistry."

I walked back over to the table and took my seat, noticing a bowl of filled with candy.

"They're hot cinnamon," Jett said. That explained the hints of cinnamon I'd detected on his breath. He must have just finished one himself. "They look like they might be peppermint," he added, "but they're not. Take one if you'd like."

"Okay." I hated that he caught me looking at them. First dinner and now this? I was starting to wonder if he viewed me as one of the "less fortunate" his father always preached about. But the fact was, I didn't want corndog breath so I snatched one, unwrapped it, and stuck it in my mouth.

Jett turned the laptop screen so it faced me this time. "Want to work your magic?" He reached for a notepad and began scribbling out a few notes.

"Sure," I said. I grabbed my backpack and retrieved a notepad of my own, along with my favorite purple pen. I typed in the words *why do people kiss* and hit enter.

"Oh, that's good," he said. "I should have searched for it that way."

I tucked the candy in my cheek so I could speak. "What did you type in?"

"About kissing."

"Those two words? About kissing?" I glanced over in time to catch a hint of color appear in his cheeks.

"Yeah. Is that lame?"

I shrugged and set my eyes back on the screen. Now that I wasn't starving anymore—in fact, I was more satisfied than I'd been in a long time—I could smell Jett's incredible spicy cologne. I felt him looking at me too. I couldn't decide if I liked that or hated it.

"Here's one," I said. "About why kissing feels so good." I felt myself blush after saying the mere title. How was I supposed to read this one aloud? Getting rid of the candy was a good place to start. I crunched it up (an act my mom swears will make my teeth fall out) and took a quick gulp of water. I clicked, sighed out a deep breath, and began to read.

The article started with a few facts like the ones Jett read, but soon it moved onto possible reasons humans were so attached to the activity in the first place. My palms grew sweaty as I spotted the next line. This was starting to feel a little...personal, but there was no going back.

"'The combination of abundant nerves and thin skin make the lips more sensitive than most areas of the body. In fact, there are more...'" I tried not to trip over the word, "'*neurotransmitters* in the lips than in the genitals.'"

"Wow," Jett said with a laugh. "Glad my dad didn't walk in and overhear that line."

I glanced over at him, laughter bubbling up my throat. "No kidding." I set my eyes back on the article, pausing for a moment to find my place, when suddenly Jett picked up where I left off.

"'The sensation of kissing sends signals to the brain's reward and pleasure centers, unleashing a spectrum of neurotransmitters and hormones. These are so powerful they can cause addiction and even withdrawl.'"

Hearing those words in the masculine tone of his voice sent a ton of transmitters into motion in my own brain. In fact, I felt it everywhere.

"Oh, this is interesting," he said. "'The first draw of a kiss just might be traced to the fact that women often paint their lips a shade of red, a color which men are often attracted to.'" He glanced over, his gaze meeting my eyes, which made me realize how very close we'd gotten. His face was mere inches from mine.

I watched as his gaze dropped to my lips. I tried to remind myself of what the article said. Something about lipstick. Was he checking to see if I'd worn any? I *had* put on a color stain. One that would stay right in place and not even smudge. But it wasn't red by any means—pink was more like it. *Frosty Rose,* that was the name of it.

Jett shook his head, an absent-looking motion, and turned back to the screen. I decided I should have been taking notes on that, so I grabbed my notebook and scribbled some of the things he'd said.

He read a bit more, something about a smelling test

suggesting that women were attracted to men who had a difference in MHC which, from what I understood, had something to do with one's immune system. The women from the study were attracted to men whose immune systems carried what theirs lacked, meaning their babies would have even stronger immune systems.

"Huh," Jett said as he leaned back into his seat. "Guess that's a little different from the *romantic chemistry* Tolken was talking about."

"Yeah," I said. "To think I could be drawn to some guy, all because he was going to help me make healthy babies one day…"

Jett chuckled. "Yeah. Pretty crazy." He was holding my gaze again. "But I liked the part that talked about, you know, how good it feels to kiss. I mean, it feels good to *me*, but I like knowing that it feels good for women too." He shrugged with just one shoulder.

I wanted to speak up and say that yes, it was true. But I hadn't had the best experiences so far, so I just nodded instead. When that didn't feel like enough, I added to it. "Yup."

Jett tilted his head, seeming to study my face.

"What?" I asked. Dang; my cheeks were going pink, I could feel it.

"You don't like kissing," he accused.

"Yes, I do."

He shook his head, still reading my face like it was the latest game plan. "No, you don't." He nodded as if I'd actually given him confirmation. "Huh, that's too bad."

"*What's* too bad?" Now my defenses were picking up.

This was the pompous Jett I remembered. Heat spread over the back of my shoulders.

Jett leaned back in the chair and folded his arms. "The fact that you're dating a guy who doesn't know the right way to kiss a woman."

Woman? Technically I was still in high school and hadn't exactly considered myself to be an official woman yet, but that didn't stop the odd thrill that shot through me. "So you're so confident, are you? About your kissing ability?"

A triumphant grin spread over his face. "Yes."

"How? How can you be sure?" I don't know why, but suddenly I started to feel like I needed a little space, so I scooted my chair back a foot or two. It didn't feel like such a weird thing to do until Jett stared down at the space between us with a furrowed brow.

Slowly then, he pulled away from the back of the chair, leaned forward to drop his elbows to his knees, and squared a good, hard look at me. "That's a good question."

A blast of firecracker-heat flared in my chest. Just where was he going with this? But then every fiber in me threatened to go limp as I realized *exactly* where he was going with it.

"How about we let *you* be the judge?"

Jett Bryant was actually asking me to kiss him. I couldn't have anticipated the kind of euphoria that spilled over me at the thought. I wanted to bask in this moment. This wasn't a game of me chasing him. This was, finally, him chasing me.

I had to wonder if all this talk of kissing was playing

tricks on us. Because all I could picture in that moment was me leaning forward, him wrapping his hands around my waist, and the two of us locking lips in a passionate, movie-worthy kiss.

I heard the slam of a car door. Not a distant one either. Seconds later came the squeaking sound of a swinging door. "Hello?"

I widened my eyes at Jett to get him to…stop leaning in and staring at me like this. His dad would think we were up to something.

Jett only grinned. "Hi Dad," he called. Still leaning over. Still staring right at me with a challenging grin.

"How's the homework coming?"

I pulled my gaze off Jett and gave Pastor Bryant a wave. It felt weird being in his home suddenly. Especially considering the conversation I'd just been having with his son.

"What is it you two are studying?" He leaned to one side to take a look at the screen. "Oh yeah, the kiss. That's an interesting topic."

Jett finally straightened up. "It sure is," he said, stretching his arms over his head.

The pastor gave my arm a nudge with the back of his hand and nodded to his son. "You don't have to kiss this kid in order to get an A do you?"

"Huh?" I squeaked.

He broke into a smile. "Kidding," he said with a laugh. He walked over to the counter and looked at the food on the tray. "Think the girls will have already eaten again?" he asked, glancing up at Jett.

Jett yawned, his biceps popping as he propped his hands behind his head. "Probably."

"Yeah. I'll get this put away. You two go on with your studies. Don't mind me."

"Well, we would, Dad," Jett said, setting his gaze back on me, "but our research actually *does* involve kissing, so I think that'd be a little awkward."

"Ah," Pastor Bryant said with a nod. "Are you sure you don't want a different partner, Harper?"

I laughed. Partly out of nerves and partly because it was actually funny. I really *had* pleaded with Ms. Tolken regarding the issue.

"Actually," Jett said with a grin. "She *did* ask for another partner. Tolken said no."

"Ha ha," his dad said. "Well, at least you tried."

I shot to my feet. "I've got to get going," I announced. It came out as awkward as it felt but I didn't care. Any minute, Pastor Bryant would disappear and I'd be stuck sitting alone with Jett and his seriously tempting offer to see for myself whether he really was a good kisser.

"I hope I didn't scare you away." His dad piled the corndogs, french fries, and pizza pockets into one big storage bag and zipped it up.

"No, you didn't. I just…remembered I was supposed to be home by…" I had no idea what time it was so I just said, "…by, um, now."

"Okay then," the man said pleasantly.

Jett didn't let me off so easily. He reached his foot out and bumped my shoe. "By *what* time?"

I glared at him, hoping he'd let it drop.

"What time was it that she told you to be home?" he repeated under his breath.

I glanced over my shoulder to see Pastor Bryant rinsing an apple at the sink. Wasn't there a microwave over there too? Yes, green glowing numbers that read five after nine.

"By nine o'clock actually," I said, "but she won't mind if I'm home a little late."

I stuffed my notes back into my bag, zipped it up, and scooted my chair back into place. Jett came to a stand and shut his laptop. "I'll walk you out." He rested his hand on my lower back, causing a sensation of tingles to move over my skin.

"That's my boy," Pastor Bryant said. He gave us a wave and bit into the apple.

"Should we, um, do this at your place next time?" Jett asked while opening the door for me.

I considered it as I stepped onto the porch and shivered.

"Do you want a jacket?" Before I could answer, he bolted back inside and came out in the speed of light. "Here." He held out his letterman jacket and motioned to me with a nod.

Jett Bryant wanted me to put on his letterman jacket? Trying hard not to overthink it, I straightened my right arm and slid it into the silky sleeve. I went to slip the backpack off my shoulder but Jett was one step ahead of me. He hooked the strap with his fingers and held it out to the side as I slipped my left arm through. Instead of handing it back to me he looped it around his own massive shoulder.

He glanced up. "Clouds are gone," he said, a far off look in his eye.

The humor and playfulness were gone, causing me to remember what my mom had said about his parents being separated.

"So," he said as we walked around to the driver's side of the car. "I've got basketball practice on Mondays, Wednesdays, and Friday nights. So how's Thursday for you?"

I looked at him, thinking of how nicely this was working out; every other day was perfect. "Sounds good."

He nodded, glanced down at his feet and tipped his head to the side. "Should we do it here again or do you want to have it at your place?"

I hadn't exactly decided on that yet. If we *did* do it there, we'd need to watch a movie as well so it looked like an actual date. "We could do that, but my little sister will be there. She might be kind of a distraction."

Jett lifted his chin, then studied me as moonlight poured over his handsome face. "I don't mind kids," he finally said, voice low and raspy.

I gulped, wondering if I should just tell him about the whole fake date fiasco. Summer had said that I shouldn't while Bailey insisted I should, so I was still a little confused. "Okay," I said. "Thursday at my place."

He gave me a nod before his face turned thoughtful. "Didn't you used to work for the Sweet Water recreation? Doing, like, theater classes for the kids?"

My heart misbehaved with a little happy dance. Why

did I like it every time Jett admitted to knowing details of my life? "Yeah," I said. "And you did some coaching, right?"

The grin that pulled at those tempting lips of his said he might like it when I remembered stuff about him as well. "Right. My dad wanted me to focus on grades, so I only work there the summer now." He shrugged and added, "Plus I work a double shift at the warehouse on Saturdays."

"My mom's the same way. She pays me a decent allowance, hoping it will, in her words, 'pay off in scholarship money later.'"

"Which it *did*," Jett pointed out.

"Yep." I nodded as my face warmed. *Dang*, he was attractive. "And yours did too."

I patted my pockets for the keys and realized they were clipped to my bag. "Oh, my keys," I said, shifting to the grip he had on it. Was it just me or was he stalling?

Jett let the backpack slide off his shoulder and held it out for me by the strap.

"Thanks." I hooked it over my shoulder, sensing there was something more he wanted to say.

"Hey, umm…how long ago did your parents get divorced?"

The question made my heart hurt. Poor Jett. And his whole family for that matter. I couldn't imagine Pastor Bryant and his wife actually getting divorced. They seemed so perfect together. I forced my mind back to his question.

"My dad took off before Missy was born," I said. "So it's been about seven years now."

Jett dropped his gaze to the curb as he slid the side of his shoe against the rounded edge. "I'm sorry. That must have been hard for you guys. All of you."

I nodded, wishing I could offer some sort of comfort over whatever he was going through now, but I couldn't. Not unless he actually opened up to me about it. As far as the congregation knew, Cathy was taking care of her mother in Georgia; the last thing I wanted him to worry about was a bunch of town gossip.

When Jett didn't offer more, I hurried into the car. "Well, I'll see you tomorrow."

He nodded. "See you."

I shut the door, and Jett moved back a few steps as I roared up the engine. A million things raced through my mind as I caught sight of him in the rearview, his silhouette exuding that tall, brooding stature.

Part of me was very excited about the idea of seeing him every other night, even if it was just for some assignment. The other part of me was warring with guilt over the odd spark I felt when Jett smiled at me or held my gaze or spoke in that deep voice of his.

Sure, I was studying with Jett for school, I really was, but I was also fake-dating him to appease my mom and Jett didn't even know it.

I sighed, forced my eyes off the rearview, and asked myself one very important question: "Harper, what in the world are you doing?"

CHAPTER FIVE

"*H*ow was your date with Jett Bryant last night?" Mom asked as she shuffled into the room.

I stared at the book in front of my face, *Taming the Shrew*, as I thought about how to answer. Not that I'd been reading it. What I'd been doing, instead, is thinking back on the way Jett had practically challenged me to kiss him. Every time I replayed the scene in my mind a deep thrill shot through my body. Of *course* I felt guilty about this delicious thrill but I could hardly stop the memory from resurfacing on what seemed to be every hour on the dot.

I was about to tell my mom that the date went fine when she spoke up again, this time hollering over her shoulder. "And are you ready for your first dance class, Missy Moo Moo?"

I dragged my eyes off my book and watched her for a moment, wondering if she'd forgotten already that she'd asked me about Jett.

"I'm ready," Missy sang out. She appeared from the hallway in head-to-toe pale pink, including her tutu and slippers. She busted out a few moves that belonged more in a jazzercise class than a ballet studio but that was probably because she'd watched my mom work out to her exercise shows.

I lowered my book and watched the little twerp bop around for a minute. "Those are some pretty wild moves, sis," I said before lifting the book back to eye level.

"Why, thank you," she said. I wasn't watching her anymore, but I could tell she was still dancing since her voice bounced and bumped.

"Homework's all done, right?" my mom asked.

"Yep." And most of it really was, thanks to my daily study hall class.

"So, is TJ coming to get you soon?"

I glanced up from my book once more.

My mom's face was serious. "I don't want you two alone here, remember?"

I held her gaze a minute longer. "It's like you add a new rule about him every time. First I have to date someone in between and now we can't even hang out here when you're gone?"

The freshly trimmed ends of Mom's bob fell around her chin as her shoulders dropped. She shot me one of those *really!?* looks and sighed. "Nice try. That one's always been a rule. No being in the house alone with a boy."

"'Because you'll kiss too much," Missy chimed while shaking her bum.

I looked back to my mom. "Yes. He's coming to get me."

"And where are you going?"

I tried to put a little excitement into my voice. "He wrote a new song, I guess, so he wants me to come watch them practice."

Mom shook her head and ushered Missy into the garage. Once the door was all but closed, she spun back to me. "I'm telling you," she said under her breath. "That boy is too much like your father. You don't want to end up with a guy like him, trust me." With that, she hurried after Missy and closed the door behind her. I set my eyes back on my book but all I could see was my dad, holding my hand as I padded along the wet sand to chase the tide with him. My dad wasn't always so... troubled. He went back and forth, kind of, from what I understood.

First he was a bad boy when my mom fell for him, mainly because he drank too much, but when my mom wound up pregnant at just nineteen years old, he stepped up, sobered up, and married her. He helped raise me until I was ten years old. And even though Mom said he would come and go during that time, weaving in and out of addiction, I had a ton of happy memories with him. But something about those memories hurt too.

My book fell to my lap as I admitted that the hurt far outweighed the joy they brought. He'd kind of ruined them by choosing to leave and not come back while my mom was pregnant with Missy. What kind of person did that? I've gone from hating him for it to blaming my mom for doing something to chase him away, to then blaming myself for doing something to chase him out of our lives.

But all of those things were just too painful and unsettling and far too flawed for me to accept, so I decided that he was actually a very good guy with a problem that might have been solved had someone just... stepped in a little sooner and held him accountable for his behavior. I'd read a million articles on addiction and the early starts.

A lot of people were just trying to fill some sort of void. What if the void in his heart could have been filled by a fulfilling job where he enjoyed what he did? Something consistent. Something he could be proud of.

I abandoned my book and took care of a few items on Mom's list. After much begging and pleading, she'd picked up some prepackaged goodies that I could pop in the microwave and dip in condiments like the rest of the universe. They were semi-gross versions of the real thing since they lacked preservatives and things like that but they were a far cry from the casserole that had scarred my kissing life with TJ.

*How about we let you be the judge...*I couldn't help but picture the smoldering look on Jett's face as he'd challenged me. My heart fluttered out of beat as heat swooshed to every limb. What did it say about me that that was possibly the most thrilling moment of my life so far?

A knock sounded at the door then, and I scrambled to rinse my plate and put it in the dishwasher. I also scrambled to shove my thoughts of Jett into a special place of their own. One I should vow not to revisit.

I swung open the door to reveal the sight of my handsome boyfriend. Blond, shaggy hair hung around his unshaven face. His blue eyes lit up as he grinned at me. "Hey."

"Hi!" I held up a finger, dashed to the bathroom, and quickly brushed my teeth, taking extra care to get my tongue too. I hurried back to the doorway and said, "Ready."

TJ grinned as I tossed my arms around him. He was so good. He liked me. He was doing his best in life. Working hard. Taking extra shifts—well, he *would* do that once he stopped calling in sick. He caught me and spun in place before setting me back down on the porch. At once he moved in for a kiss. I prepared myself by keeping a tight pucker; I wasn't ready for a repeat of yesterday.

TJ didn't exactly take the hint. He pulled me a bit tighter and tipped his head to one side. His tongue nudged my lip. For a split second, I wondered if I just give in and see if this time could be better. But I chickened out and pulled back instead; I did *not* want TJ to prove Jett right about the whole kissing thing.

"So how was your day?" I chirped. "I really missed hanging out with you yesterday."

TJ tossed his arm around me and nodded toward the old Chevy. "I missed you too. We just jammed most of the day. After work, that is."

I sighed in relief. See, he was doing so well.

"I mean, I was a tiny bit late 'cause we kind of partied

last night. But a bunch of people came to watch this time. It was awesome. Felt like we were performing on stage or something."

I shivered against the breeze as the words *kind of partied* ran through my mind. TJ rushed around to his side of the Chevy as I cranked open the passenger side and climbed in. Once he was settled behind the wheel, I spoke up once more, reminding myself that I did not want to lecture him. "Who was all there? Anyone I know?"

"Uh, a few of the MG's came. Couple of their jock friends too."

The seatbelt strap was only halfway across my lap but I paused at this news and turned to him. "You invited the mean girls?"

"Jessie did, but yeah. They're not that bad."

A vision of Tasha shot to my mind. Her bright red, venomous lips as she spread on yet another coat of lipstick while glaring my way. "Which girls were there?"

TJ checked his rearview and pulled onto the road. "Can't remember all their names. Olivia, Stacy, I think. Jenny..."

I nodded. Jenny and Stacy were Tasha's sidekicks. Two of the girls who'd been giggling in the corner of the locker room to egg Tasha on. Thank heavens Jett was free from her.

"That Tasha chick was there too," he said. "And it's funny because she used to date Jett Bryant, and *you* were with *him* last night, and *I* was with *her*."

"You were *with her* last night?" I squeaked. "I thought

CHEMISTRY OF A KISS

you said everybody was there." The back of my shoulders turned fire hot in a blink.

"We were. At first. But then she stuck around for a while and asked where you were, so..."

That wasn't even a normal place to drift off. "So *what?*"

"So I told her that you were, like, gonna have to see other people."

Wow, the conversation was getting more annoying by the minute. "Did you misunderstand what my mom said?" I shifted in the seat. "She didn't say I needed to start *seeing other people*. She only said that I couldn't go out with you until I, you know..."

"Saw another guy in between," he said flatly. "Which is the same thing as seeing other people."

The angry heat was climbing right up my neck already. "Yeah, but I'm not actually *dating* someone else. We're partners in class. I'm doing homework with the *pastor's* son." There. That should shed a little light on things.

"Yeah, well Jett's not Mr. Innocent or anything." TJ shook his head, and I noticed his jaw tighten. "Anyway, if you're going to keep seeing Jett, we figured we'd just hang out together too on those nights."

My ears had a hard time taking that in. I leaned in to get a better look at TJ's face. "*Who* is going to get together? And why are you making me work so hard to pry this conversation out of you?"

"Me and Tasha. It was *her* idea, but I think it's a good one."

"Oh, are you kidding? Yeah, that's the best idea I can possibly think of. You should totally spend your time with a girl who will help you throw your life down the drain as quickly as possible."

TJ shook his head. "You're just jealous."

Of *course* I was jealous. Freaking Tasha was making the moves on yet another guy I liked. How could two completely opposite girls be attracted to the same two completely opposite guys? Of course, it made more sense for Tasha to like TJ than it did for me. But that was the problem. I didn't want him to be influenced by someone like her.

I folded my arms and sank back into the seat. My hopes of a sober, happy TJ were being ripped from my grasp at lightning speed and there was nothing I could do to stop it. Hot tears stung my eyes. I didn't want to lose him. I didn't want to let go.

Those exact thoughts replayed in my mind as I watched my own proverbial untamed shrew tip back drinks and pour his heart out over the mic. At one point, he inserted my name into one of the songs, *"Harper, why'd you have to hurt me this way?"*

He followed the action with a charismatic wink that made me want to cry. If I left TJ, I really *would* hurt him— in more ways than one. It could affect his entire future.

When the night was through, I got a ride home from Jessie, the one member of the band who didn't drink. I wasted no time tossing my clothes in the hamper and climbing under the sheets. I stayed awake with anxious thoughts of TJ, tears soaking into my pillowcase as the hours trudged by. One vision stood out among the rest, and it haunted me all the way to my core. I envisioned headlines splashed all over the country: *Famous Rock Star, TJ Reynolds, Found Dead in His NY Apartment at the Young Age of Twenty-Four.*

That did it. Forget about Jett and his luscious lips and alluring eyes. I needed to keep my sights on TJ. He needed a girl like me, and I wouldn't let him down.

CHAPTER SIX

"What time is Jett coming to pick you up tonight?"

Mom's question hit my ears the moment I spotted Missy parade into the kitchen wearing her frilly layers of pink.

"You can't be in the house alone while we're gone," Mom added in my silence.

A beat of panic thrummed in my chest. "Wait, I thought she had dance class on Wednesdays and Fridays," I said.

Missy put her hands over her head and popped herself onto the balls of her feet. "Nope," she sang.

"It's Wednesdays and *Thursdays*," Mom corrected.

I stared at the pan of health-freak brownies I just pulled from the oven and sighed. "I thought we were going to be able to study here."

"Study?" A layer of shock coated the word. "You're doing a study date?"

My face shifted into busted-mode but I quickly worked up enough of a cough to clear my throat. "Well, yeah, he's the captain of the basketball team. The guy has to keep his grades up."

Mom tipped her head, thoughtful, as her eyes seemed to land on Missy and her dance moves. A wobbly spin in the center of the plush rug.

Maybe now was my chance. "Besides," I added, "it's not like he's going to, like, *try* anything while you're gone."

The words floated there for a while before I got my reply.

"Why? Just because he's the pastor's son? That one's not going to work on me. No being in the house alone with a boy. That's final."

The word *boy* sounded just fine when she'd said it about TJ, so why now did it seem inadequate when describing Jett, who was a year younger than him?

"Come on, Missy Moo." Mom hiked her massive purse over her shoulder and ushered Missy toward the door. "When does play practice start up for you?" she asked as she yanked open the garage door.

"We started practicing on the first day in school," I said, knowing it wasn't the answer she was looking for.

Mom tucked the blonde strands of her bob behind one ear and sighed. "I mean the after school practices."

"After Thanksgiving," I said.

Mom punched the garage button and spoke loudly

over the motorized growl. "I mean it about no boys in the house. Have fun."

I stared at the kitchen table. I'd spent, like, twenty minutes getting the floor swept and another twenty minutes getting Missy's art supplies tucked into the corner of the cabinet all while a pan of brownies baked in the oven and hopefully made this place at least smell like a normal home. Anything to get the scent of Mom's cabbage soup out of here. All to find out that my mom wasn't playing favorites or reserving certain rules for certain guys.

A thick knot of dread ripped through me as I recalled the rough night I'd had with TJ. First the date, then the stream of nightmares about his fate. I hated thinking he was destined for tragedy. And just what was I supposed to do about this whole study date? Maybe it was time to tell Jett about my secret agenda. He wouldn't like it, but hopefully he'd be understanding. I sighed as I made my way to the pantry. There was one last thing on my list of chores and that was to take out the trash.

I snatched the brownie box off the top of the heap, realizing I should've put it in the recycling, and cinched the white bag nice and tight. With a quick tug, I hoisted the thing out of the tall, plastic bin and made my way to the front door. I was just about to tuck the brownie box under my arm and twist the knob when a sharp rap of knocks sounded from the other side.

I stared at the white door for a blink. "Come in," I chimed.

The silver knob twisted. The door creaked open. And

there stood a sight that made me recall the very scene I'd banned from my brain—the recollection of Jett leaning forward, looking at me with those smoldering eyes, and practically daring me to kiss him.

I blinked, reminding myself that he was *not* daring me to kiss him now. "Hi," I managed.

He grinned. "Hi there." At once his eyes darted to the bag in my grip. "Here, let me get that for you." He pried the bag from my fingers before I could protest and turned right back out the door.

I followed him as he strode to the garbage, pried the lid open, and flung it inside. He proceeded to grip the handle in back and walk it to the curb without a second thought. Of course, if it was garbage night here it was garbage night in all of Sweet Water, so he knew the drill, but I couldn't exactly stop myself from *really really really* liking the way Jett had stepped up and helped me without asking. No wonder moms liked it so much.

"Recycle?" Jett asked, pulling me from my stupor.

I looked down at the box in my hand and nodded.

"Here." He held his hand out and I handed it over like a zombie robot and watched the way he tore open the ends, flattened it, and strode to the recycle bin where he tossed it in.

"Thanks." The word fell off my lips as he dusted his hands on his jeans. Black jeans. They looked nice with his ashy gray V-neck tee. Gracious, he looked like a walking advertisement for aftershave for crying out loud. My heart kicked out a few extra beats in double rhythm.

He started back toward the house next. I hurried

alongside, assembling the words in my head. "My mom won't let us be in the house alone," I said.

Jett stopped walking. "She's not home?"

I shook my head. "I didn't realize it, but Missy has dance lessons tonight, so..."

"That makes sense. At least she acknowledges that I'm a normal guy. I hate when parents assume I'm going to be perfect just because I'm the pastor's son."

A guilty gulp slunk down my throat. "Is this a bad time to admit that I actually tried to play that card with her?"

Jett's face turned thoughtful. He lifted one dark brow and stepped close enough for me to smell that yummy spicy scent on him, giving life to that whole aftershave advertisement thought. I eyed the very slight hint of a five o'clock shadow along his jaw and gulped once more.

"How come?"

His question took me off guard. I could barely hear it over the rapid thumps in my chest. "Huh?"

"Why did you try to play that card with your mom?" A smile tugged at one side of his full lips. "You *wanted* to be alone in the house with me?"

My eyes widened a second before I slapped his arm. "No. Sheesh. I just...wanted to actually get some work done. But don't worry, my mom was adamant—no special treatment for you in the Tisdale home," I assured. I could hear how strained my own voice sounded after the wanting to be alone with him accusation but there was nothing I could do about it. The fact was, I'd been accidentally fantasizing about what it might feel like to have him kiss me on the couch for the last two days.

"Good." A cryptic grin tugged at Jett's lips. "I'm not as innocent as moms like to think I am." The statement seemed to ignite flames in my cheeks.

His gaze shifted to my house. A furrow creased his brow as he studied it, as if the bright red bricks and white pillars held the solution. "My sisters are hosting some sort of watch party at my place," he said, "but we could try to sneak into the den." He scratched the side of his face. "My dad wouldn't like that though…"

The moment was presenting itself, wasn't it? I should just tell him that I was using our study dates to make it look like I was seeing someone between my nights with TJ. I tried to work up the courage. "We could go grab a shake," I suggested. Maybe working up to it was best. "At the Burger Bar they have wifi. Sometimes." I added the *sometimes* in there because half the time it didn't work all that well. "If it's working tonight, we could do a little research in the car."

"Their wifi never works," he said, eyes still set on my house. Perhaps he'd been thinking of that couch kiss as well. His gaze shifted back to me, his expression still puzzled. "You trying to get out of doing homework tonight?"

I felt caught suddenly. I shrugged.

He eased back into that smile. "All right," he said, tucking his hand into his pocket and retrieving his keys. "Burger Bar it is."

I told myself, while sitting beside Jett in his black pickup truck, that I needed to just fess up about the dating thing, but by the time the Burger Bar came into view I decided it was too late. My eyes wandered over the large crowd outside the small shack. The Burger Bar wasn't your typical restaurant with indoor tables and vinyl booths. Customers walked up to the ordering windows, listed their picks from the menu, and waited for their number to be called. While there were a few outdoor benches cornering the property, most people took their food back to the dirt lot where they piled into cars or sat in the backs of their pickup trucks while they ate.

Jett turned and asked what I wanted as he ordered, but I shook my head and insisted I pay for myself. Forget the fact that I'd just made brownies for the first time ever. They were probably gross anyway. I stepped over to the window beside Jett's and placed an order of my own—a cookie dough shake and a large fry.

"We're running a little behind," Troy Ingleson said as he handed over my number.

I glanced down at the circled digits on my receipt. "Thanks."

"You going to Sadies?" Troy asked next.

I tore my gaze from the receipt to take in Troy's wide grin. Were those new braces? Sadies, short for Sadie Hawkins, was one of Sweet Water's girl's choice dances. "I'm not sure," I said. "TJ doesn't exactly like school dances, so…"

Troy nodded. "Sweet Water probably wouldn't let him in, anyway. Think you're supposed to be a high schooler still. I haven't been asked yet."

I blinked. Why did it feel like this kid was asking me to ask him? "Huh. Hope someone asks you," I managed with a nod. Man, was the Sadie's dance coming up so soon? I was supposed to help the theater department make posters for it. But who knew if I'd actually be showing up to the thing myself. It was just one more way that TJ stood out from the crowd, and not in a good way. Why couldn't he just be a normal kid and do normal things like go to dances and lead up to a kiss slowly like he was supposed to?

I spun around to see Jett waiting for me beside the large oak tree. I looked at the ground as I walked toward him, feeling the awkwardness of the moment times ten. I wanted to pretend that this was normal and that we were just a couple of friends getting together to do homework and have a shake, but ever since Jett sort of dared me to kiss him, the guy roused too many conflicting emotions in me.

I stopped walking once I was about a yard away and glanced up to see his face. Yep. Still gorgeous. Annoyingly so. It seemed almost cruel for someone to be that...attractive.

"What'd you order?" he asked.

"Cookie dough shake. Fries. You?"

He grinned. "Mint shake with tots."

"Mmm," I said. "I used to get mint every time."

He grinned. "You did? Until when?"

I folded my arms as a breeze blew in. "Until I tried cookie dough," I said with a laugh.

Jett lifted a brow. "That good, huh? You'll have to let me taste it."

I felt my eyes widen in surprise as I tried to picture

what that would look like. Me scooping a heap onto my spoon and feeding it to him? Or would he simply reach in with his own spoon and take a sample for himself?

"What the ..." Jett's eyes hardened suddenly. I stared at him, watching as his gaze followed a trail from the lot to the ordering window. I was about to turn around and see who was here for myself when Jett's gaze shifted back to me. The angry scowl hadn't left his face yet but I somehow knew it wasn't meant for me.

An odd dose of anticipation skittered over my skin as I spun to look over my shoulder. At first glance, I noticed a bunch of kids our age, but as I took a longer look, I realized it was the crew from Jessie's garage. There was Jessie, Dino, and...*Tasha?*

A sudden wave of nausea flared as I realized who she was cuddled up to. *Really* cuddled up to: TJ. There he was, ordering at the window while Tasha snuggled her face into his chest. Which meant those hands resting very closely to her rear end were TJ's.

"You've got to be kidding." I turned away from the sight and shook my head. What was going on here?

Jett stepped closer to me. "Are you two broken up?" he asked under his breath.

I glanced up, moved by the intensity I saw on his face. "Not exactly."

"Then what the crud is he doing?"

I sank my face into my palm and shrugged. "I've got no idea." Except that was only partway true. Sure, TJ said that while I study with Jett, he and Tasha might hang out.

72

Hanging out was different from hanging all over each other.

"Do you want to go confront him?" Jett asked.

I didn't bother pulling my face away. "No," I mumbled against my hand.

"Do you want *me* to confront him?" he asked.

This time I pulled my hand away, and quick. "No," I assured, surprised that he'd offered. Later I'd have to ask him what that would have entailed. But right now, I had to decide what to do. I imagined the newspaper article once more, thinking of how much closer TJ seemed to that gone-too-soon rock star fate with his little crony, Tasha, at his hip.

"Tasha's pathetic," Jett growled.

And that's when it hit me. Jett was jealous. Tasha was his ex-girlfriend, after all. I wondered how jealous TJ might be if he saw me cuddled up to Jett. Would it be enough for him to call off this side thing with Tasha and commit to only me? But then another question came to mind: Would Jett be interested in making Tasha jealous in return?

I shuffled closer to Jett, testing, and wondered if he would play along.

He didn't move, only stayed in place as I closed the gap enough that the toe of my shoes grazed his.

"Are you cold?" he asked under his breath. And then his hands were sliding up my arms, warm and strong and assuring.

Goosebumps spread over my skin at his touch. My heart must have had them too because suddenly it skipped a few beats. A crazy amount of tingly euphoria rushed through me from being so close to him. "A little," I said, reveling in the feel of it.

"Come here." Jett wrapped his arms around me and encouraged me even closer. Tentatively, I allowed my arms to wrap around him in return.

More euphoria. Lots of it.

I'd heard the term blurred lines in my life, but only in that moment did I understand what it meant. I wasn't sure if I was getting closer to make TJ jealous, or because a part of me had never stopped liking Jett.

He was just so warm and tempting and yummy-smelling.

Suddenly his lip grazed my ear.

I stiffened as every inch of me keyed into the sensation of his hot breath tickling my skin. Another round of goosebumps raced up my arms.

"Now might be a good time to take me up on that dare," he said into my ear.

Whoa. As if I hadn't been picturing that very thing since he'd posed the dare in the first place. Of course I would never really kiss Jett while I was dating TJ, but the suggestion was toying with my head.

I lifted my chin, heart pounding its wild beat, and locked my gaze on Jett's deep brown eyes.

Suddenly a voice sounded from the fuzzy-sounding speakers behind me. "Number eighty-six and eighty-seven, your orders are ready."

Jett cleared his throat and straightened. "That's me. Are you number eighty-seven?"

I stepped away from him, trying to shake off all the tingles from his touch, and reached into my back pocket for my receipt. A quick glance at the slip confirmed it. "Yeah." I spun around, anxious to see if we'd been spotted by TJ. It took a moment to place them since they weren't at the ordering counter anymore. They'd made their way over to the bench. TJ was looking in my direction, but I couldn't be sure that he saw me. And what was this? Tasha was making herself comfortable on his lap.

Anger burned up the back of my shoulders as I followed Jett to the pickup counter. Tasha raked her hand through TJ's hair next. The action had me so captured I ran right into Jett.

"Sorry," I mumbled the word without taking my eyes off the sight. Blindly, I slapped my receipt down on the counter and felt around for the Styrofoam cup.

"I've already got it," Jett said. "Let's go."

Tasha was moving in for a kiss. I couldn't believe my eyes. She was actually moving in for a kiss! And...and TJ went for it!

"Harper," Jett said under his breath. "Let's go."

I tore my eyes from the nasty sight and looked up at Jett. The clenched set of his jaw said he didn't like what he'd seen any more than I did. With a shake in each hand, he nodded toward the lot.

"Yeah," I managed. "We better go." I sped ahead of him toward the truck, stopping only as I waited for Jett to catch up. He came around to the passenger side and lifted my shake toward me. I took it, noticing then that he had a white paper bag too. Must be our fries and tots.

"Thanks," I said, taking it from him while he opened the door for me. I climbed in, knowing Jett had seen what I had, dreading the conversation that was sure to come. *"I told ya you can't change people."* Or *"You're stupid to waste your time with that jerk."*

Jett climbed in behind the wheel and set his shake in the cup holder. "Want to get out of here?" he asked.

A deep sense of sadness gripped hold of me as I nodded yes. I couldn't figure out what was going on inside of me. It felt like I was accepting failure in one sense, or at least trying to, while dealing with a crapload of humiliation at the same time.

"I'm sorry," Jett mumbled as he tore out of the lot and onto the road.

I clenched my eyes shut. "He's mad that I'm seeing you," I explained. And since I'd opened the door, I decided to keep going. "My little sister caught me and TJ kissing, and she told on me. So my mom said that if I wanted to keep seeing TJ, I'd have to date someone else in between." I risked a glance over at Jett.

He gave me a quick nod, a handsome furrow pulling at that brooding brow of his.

"So I figured, since you and I were doing homework anyway, I could, you know, sort of count that as *seeing* another guy in between." My half-broken heart picked up its pace once more. I felt like a big liar, but technically I wasn't, was I?

"Does TJ know about it? The fact that you have to see someone else?"

"Yeah. In fact, just last night he told me that Tasha

came out and watched him sing with Grunge Town in Jessie's garage, and they were sparking up some stupid plan to, you know, see each other while you and I were together on the off nights."

"I should have kissed you," he spat.

I was pretty sure my heart stopped beating altogether. Tingly heat danced circles around the failing vessel. "Excuse me?"

"We should've given those idiots a taste of their own medicine, not just skulked off like a couple of losers."

Skulk?

"And you know, Tasha, she banks on me being the tame one, right? She's thinking, '*Oh, Jett's too much of a gentleman to do anything to Harper in public.*' But what I should have done is back you against that tree and given *them* something to talk about."

A million receptors were scurrying throughout my entire body at the image he'd painted in my head. I was trying to have a pity party for myself but how could I when the kid I'd had a not-so-secret crush on since kindergarten was talking about backing me against trees and giving my cheating boyfriend and his ex-girlfriend something to talk about?

"I mean, is this his way of saying we're, like, officially seeing other people or what?" I blurted. "And did you see how *disgusting* that kiss looked?" I couldn't believe I was actually going there, but I was, and there was no stopping me.

I shifted in the seat and faced Jett's shadowed profile as I continued. "I was trying to be nice the other night when

I was acting like I enjoyed TJ's kiss, but the truth is, he is the sloppiest, anxious...est, grossest kisser on the planet." I rode on the high that came from bashing TJ and his stupid cheating self.

I waited for Jett to step up and do the same, but he only gripped the wheel and shook his head. His jaw was clenched tight; perhaps he was holding back the words.

"Tasha didn't look like the world's best kisser either," I said, gearing him in the right direction. Heck, we were practically experts on the subject right? *We* were the ones studying the chemistry of a kiss.

"Tasha's not bad. She was probably just adjusting to his kissing style. They say that's what's best so you can, you know, get into a good groove."

I sat there, lips parted, poised to say something, but for the life of me I couldn't think of what. I felt miffed. Just what made Jett the expert? "Sounds like someone's been doing a little research without me," I suggested.

Jett chuckled under his breath and glanced over. "Truth? I have twin sisters who subscribe to chick magazines. When I was dating Becky Wilson during freshman year, I noticed a few of the articles were about kissing. What to do. What *not* to do. How to train clueless guys to settle down a little." He shrugged. "I studied up."

Lucky Becky. And just what in the world was Jett trying to do to me anyway?

It remained quiet as he drove straight to the Sweet Water Church. I glanced up at the illuminated chapel, raising a brow as he pulled into the vacant lot.

"Free wifi," Jett explained. He shut off the engine,

cracked open his door, and climbed out. I watched as he proceeded to retrieve a blanket from the back cab, and then his backpack. "I've got a jacket for you, if you'd like."

He held it up, reminding me of the letterman jacket I had hanging on my bedpost. (Don't judge.) I managed a nod, and Jett handed it over before tossing the blanket into the flatbed.

I unlatched my seatbelt and helped out by grabbing the goods from the Burger Bar. Like the gentleman he was, Jett helped me into the bed of the truck. We finished our shakes while watching a few videos about kissing on his laptop. I offered to take notes in Jett's notebook since I hadn't brought my own, and that's what I did. It was more of a robotic action, of course, since my mind was scattered in a million directions. I basically just wrote repeats of things I heard on the video word for word.

Physical changes that take place as we anticipate a kiss. *Pupils dilate. Cheeks and face flush with heat. Pulse races. Nostrils flare slightly.*

The next video spoke more about recognizing signs that your date wants to kiss. I jotted those down as well. *Holds eye contact. Gets closer. Looks at lips. Draws attention to own lips.*

I inwardly knew I wasn't great company, but Jett didn't seem to mind. In fact, I realized as we packed up and prepared to leave that he was stuck in his head too. It wasn't until he pulled into my driveway that he hinted to the thoughts that were keeping him.

"Maybe we should give them a taste of their own medicine."

I tore my gaze off our flickering porch light (I'd have to replace that) and turned to Jett.

He shifted in his seat. "Come to my locker tomorrow morning and we'll give Tasha a show of her own." A spark of determination lit those brown eyes of his, visible even in the low light.

I was pretty sure fireworks were going off somewhere in my chest at the mere suggestion. A HUGE part of me liked what he was saying. Really liked it. But there was another part of me, somewhere, trying desperately to speak up about the fact that…that Jett might still really like Tasha. It was a stupid thing to get stuck on at a moment like this. After all, I had TJ, didn't I? Or *did* I?

"I don't know," I finally said. "This is starting to get messy. I just…I'm genuinely trying to be a good girlfriend here. I honestly thought I could just let my study dates with you count, make my mom *and* TJ happy, and then he had to go and mess it all up."

Jett stared at me for a blink, then he nodded. "Just think about it." He unlatched his seatbelt then and climbed out of the truck. I watched as he circled the thing and opened my door as well. He offered me his hand next.

I took it, trying to ignore the tingles at his touch, and climbed down. I freed my hand once my feet hit the ground, and tucked a strand of hair behind my ear. I appreciated the fact that Jett was willing to walk me to the door, evident by the way he started heading down the walkway with me, but I was too anxious to get inside and work through the mess in my mind. Plus, if Jett's lips tempted me even one more time before I could sort out this whole thing with TJ, I'd feel even worse.

So I darted ahead of him, took the steps in two quick lunges, and turned back to see him standing on the walkway. "See you in class," I said, and pulled open the door.

Jett gave me a wave from where he stood. "Tomorrow."

CHAPTER SEVEN

I had barely fallen asleep that night when a series of *pings* woke me up. Woodchips hitting my window. I recognized the sound since TJ had come over past bedtime once before.

Still half asleep, I shuffled over to the french doors and pushed open the drapes. Yards below, TJ stood on the lawn, his tall figure illuminated by the flickering porch light. He waved a long, skinny arm.

I sighed and motioned him up. May as well get this over with now. My bedroom was—like all of the bedrooms in the colonial style home—on the second floor. But TJ was tall enough to reach the banister of the small deck. I unlocked the door, twisted the knob to crack it open, and hurried back over to my bed.

While I waited for TJ to let himself in, I thought back on the way he'd kissed Tasha earlier. I'd learned back in girl scouts that every fire needed fuel to feed the flames. That kiss was all the fuel I needed.

I grit my teeth as I heard him grunting his way over the banister. A loud thump told me his landing on the balcony hadn't been too cushy. *Good.* My eyes were adjusting to the lack of light in the room. Enough that when TJ stepped inside, closing the door behind him, I could see his figure from head to toe.

"Hi," he rasped.

"What are you doing here, TJ?" I asked, straightening my shoulders and lifting my chin.

"Tasha said she saw you guys at the Burger Bar."

The comment took me by surprise. "And you didn't?" Sure, I hadn't made eye-contact with him or anything, but I was pretty sure he'd seen me there.

"No, I swear. I totally didn't even know you guys were there." He broke into a pace. "And suddenly Tasha plants this make-out kiss on me and I wasn't expecting that at all, and then she tells me that you and Jett were there but that you guys just left."

"You *kissed* her, TJ." Just hearing myself say it aloud made the ache tear through my heart once more.

TJ hung his head. "I know. I'm sorry."

"What were you *thinking?*"

"Well..." He walked over to my closet and then spun around to face me once more. "*You're* the one who said we should see other people."

Forget feeding the flame. That comment started an entirely new fire. I shot to my feet and readied myself to pull out the finger quotes. "TJ. What part of 'it was my mom's idea' do you not understand?"

"Yeah, but Tasha says that you've always wanted Jett." He yanked out the finger quotes next. "She just thinks it's pretty 'convenient' that he's the one you chose to 'study' with."

"Are you suggesting that we haven't really been studying? Because I can show you the notes." The second the words left my lips I regretted them. Our notes were centered around *kissing* of all things, and one article even managed to throw in the word genitals.

"You know what?" I blurted before he could take me up on the offer. I felt the grip I had on TJ's life, his future, his well being, slipping right from my grasp. My lip trembled as I forced out my next words. "You thought we were actually seeing other people, right? That's what you thought? That's why you kissed Tasha?"

TJ rushed in to close the gap and took hold of my elbows. "Yes. You have to believe me. That's *exactly* what I thought. But—"

"No." I threw up a hand and backed away. "That's perfect. Let's just leave it at that. We're seeing other people now." I turned away from him and hurried back to my bed. Something squeaked from the hallway, and I shot a look to my closed bedroom door. "Shh," I hissed. "We probably woke my mom up."

TJ shifted his weight from one foot to the next, head turned toward the door as well. "Or Missy," he whispered before taking slow steps toward me. He put his hands up.

"I don't *want* you to see anyone else," he said, but I steeled my resolve.

"Too bad." I folded my arms, noting how he'd said he didn't want *me* seeing anyone else. He hadn't said *he* didn't want to see other people himself. Perhaps I could use this as leverage. The moment he lost something really good by doing something dumb. Maybe it'd be motivation to change. Or maybe he'd even start doing some of the things on that list we made if he thought he could get me back somehow.

I let the idea take the lead as I spoke up once more. "I can tell you don't want a girlfriend who tries to...control your life," I said, only somehow there were tears welling up in my eyes. Breaking things off with TJ hurt more than I thought it might. Especially since I was literally letting go of whatever control I had on the choices he made. He'd probably really go crazy now.

My mind scrambled its way back to my original hope —the part that said maybe this would help him clean up his life and make a change once and for all.

"We don't have to stop seeing each other," I said softly. "But I think we should date other people too."

"Yeah," TJ growled. "You already said that." He smeared a hand over his face, shuffled back to the balcony door, and flung it open. "Have fun with *Pastor Boy.*" He left the door open behind him, allowing a cold breeze to rush into my room.

I pulled the throw off my bed and wrapped it around me, staring at the open crack. After a long while and a heartfelt prayer, I climbed off my bed and closed the door tight. I plopped onto the floor, snatched TJ's old sweatshirt off the nearby bench, and curled up to it on the floor as I fell asleep.

How was I supposed to help him now?

CHAPTER EIGHT

J spent exactly thirteen minutes in the parking lot agonizing over whether or not I should meet Jett at his locker. I kept replaying his offer in my mind. *Come to my locker tomorrow morning and we'll give Tasha a show of her own.*

A burst of warm bubbles rushed through me each time I considered it. I made up two pretty good reasons for wanting to take him up on the offer:

1. I'd like to prove to myself that I could move on from TJ.

2. I'd get a certain satisfaction out of making Tasha jealous. Obviously she wasn't over Jett if she had to kiss TJ like that right in front of his face.

But inwardly, I knew exactly why I wanted to fling open the entry to the east hall, stride over to Jett's locker, and let him plant a heavenly kiss on me. It was the same reason I'd chased him down in kindergarten. The same reason I'd beat myself up over passing on my chance to kiss him in junior high. I liked Jett Bryant.

So what was my problem? This should be perfect. I was finally getting what I wanted.

But I wasn't so sure that I was.

First of all, I had a bunch of guilt surrounding the thing with TJ. I know he was the one who kissed someone else while we were dating, but I'd been *thinking* about kissing Jett a whole lot over the last few days. If I strode right up to Jett's locker and locked lips with him now, I'd feel like a complete jerk. I should at least pause and have some sort of…grieving period, right?

Plus, as much as I wanted to kiss Jett, and I *really, really* wanted to kiss him, I needed him to want me too. If we were doing it for the sake of making Tasha and TJ jealous, Jett would be thinking of *her* instead of me. I hated that idea.

So that was final. I opted right out of that plan and walked into the school through the front entry instead, which I never do. I hoisted my backpack higher onto my shoulder and pushed my way through the swarm of band boys as they hummed out their notes in the foyer. I'd barely made it another two steps when Ms. Tolken grabbed onto my shoulder.

"Harper," she said, sounding oddly cheery. "Mr. Meadows wants you to head to the theater room to work on posters during first period. I'll mark you down as excused."

I nodded, realizing this meant I wouldn't see Jett. Relief clashed with a swelling tide of disappointment.

Man, I really was a hormonal teenager. "Okay," I said. "Thanks."

"How's your assignment coming along?" Ms. Tolken hollered over the growing noise.

I stared at her dark-rimmed glasses and chronically-bunned hair, feeling oddly transparent in the moment, as if the woman had not only hair and clothes from that of an eighty-year-old but the seasoned intuition as well.

"Good," I squeaked. "Yeah. It's a...pretty interesting topic." *Shut up, Harper!*

A spark of mischief lit the woman's eyes. "Yes," she agreed. "It is."

Huh. I'd suspected that Ms. Tolken purposely handed me that red envelope. Her reaction fed the suspicion. I doubted that she memorized every topic she gave to every set of partners in her classes. But then again, she didn't seem to have much of a life outside school besides possibly raiding garage sales at the old folk's home.

The bell rang out as I approached the opening to the east hallway. Jett would be heading to first period about now, like the rest of the school. Hopefully I wouldn't bump into him. I decided to skip the trip to my own locker and hurry to the theater room. Mr. Meadows wouldn't care if I brought my backpack.

I weaved through one cluster after the next, hoping to hurry past the intersection of halls without incident, when I spotted a sight that drew my attention like a some sort of magic lure: Jett, of course. He wore a black tee shirt today, the color making him appear all the more that tall, dark, and handsome type girls always fall for.

The thunderous booms in my chest reminded me that I hadn't actually wanted to bump into him. Especially since it was easy to see that I'd come in from the front of the school instead of the east hall where he'd wanted to hook up this morning.

"Hey," he mumbled as he passed. He was quick to set his eyes back on the distant hallway ahead of him.

I didn't bother saying it back since he was already shuffling further down the hall. Besides, I wasn't even going to class today. Would he think I was avoiding him? Part of me was, but I hadn't come up with the Sadie's posters idea. I considered that as I filtered into theater. The low rafters were set up in preparation for the set building, which should be taking place in the next few weeks.

Bailey waved me to the floor where she sat hovered over a large sheet of butcher paper. A couple dozen markers lay scattered about, reminding me of the mess Missy made at home on the daily. I hunkered down, made myself cozy beside Bailey, and went to work. Mr. Meadows had scored a few boxes of donuts, so I snatched up a powdered one with red filling and tried not to moan in ecstasy at the taste.

More students filtered into the room to help. Officers, cheerleaders, that type of thing. Thank heavens Tasha was suspended from the squad; I couldn't handle the thought of having to see her. Each group filtered into a different area of the large drama room, keeping their distance for the most part. It came to my attention, though, that one group had camped awfully close to us.

I felt my shoulders shrink a bit as I scooted back to create space. I was about to glance up and see who it was when a voice spoke up and answered the question in my head.

"Hey." The second one-word greeting he'd given that day.

I knew my eyes were wide with surprise as I shot a look at him. "Jett?" Connor and a few other guys from the team sat beside him. "What are you guys doing?"

"He's captain of the basketball team," Connor said. "Coach said we had to come help."

"Oh yeah," I said. I forced my face down and stared at the capital D I'd just traced out with my pencil.

"You guys have paints back here, don't you?" Jett asked. "*That's* something I could get into."

"Yeah," Connor agreed. "Paints are way better than markers."

Bailey tipped her head to one side and leaned far over the poster, her red marker poised over a Pearl Jam CD case she'd drawn in the corner. The theme for the year was 90's grunge. "We've got a ton of paints in back."

Jett thumped the bottom of my shoe with his. "Let's go get them."

I stared at the sign some more as Jett's suggestion sank in. What he'd said might have been innocent enough, but the insinuative tone he'd used was far from it. I glanced up at him in time to catch a sideways grin tugging at his lips. Warmth stirred in my chest. My breath hitched.

"Okay." It came out in a whisper.

Jett eased into a fuller grin, the look of triumph

evident on his face, and offered his hand. My heart did one of those melty things because I was starting to really love how chivalrous he was.

I placed my hand in his and secretly delighted in the feel of his touch. "This way," I said under my breath. I didn't exactly want to announce where we were heading because a very big part of me knew we were going backstage for more than a set of paints. That idea came to life as I pushed back the heavy black curtain and stepped into the narrow space.

I held the fabric and spun in place to let Jett in as well. He stepped through, bringing that heavenly, spicy scent with him, and a rush of magnetic energy picked up. It felt like a living force, restlessly prodding for us to act on the attraction between us. One video we'd watched just last night suggested that kissing told couples whether or not they were well matched. Not just the whole theory of healthy babies and immune systems, but actual compatibility.

I slowed my pace, somehow knowing that Jett wanted me to turn around. I wouldn't do it on my own though. If he felt what I was feeling, he'd stop me somehow. And I very much hoped that he would. I slowed my pace even more.

"Harper, wait."

The melty things exploded into little sparklers inside my chest. "Huh?" I stopped walking, spun in place, and set my eyes on Jett in the bluish gray light.

"I waited for you by my locker this morning."

I gulped.

"How come you didn't come?"

Wow. This was a forward, new Jett, wasn't it?

I shrugged.

He leaned a shoulder against the wall. "I heard you broke things off with TJ."

That surprised me. "You did?"

"Tasha texted me," he said with a nod.

The sound of her name made my shoulders tense.

"Listen …" Jett glanced at the floor for a blink. "I'm sorry that happened with TJ and Tasha last night. And I don't want to rush you or anything, but…"

Why did I like the sound of that *but* so much? Maybe it was because I'd been the one perceivably chasing him all along. First on the playground when we were six years old. Then at the party when the spinning bottle had stopped on him. Heck, if I'd been the one to walk in through those east doors and step up to Jett's locker this morning, that would have been *me* going to him once again. But if we ended up kissing right here, right now, it would be Jett initiating all of it. The idea to go get the paints was his. Stopping on the way to the stockroom where they were blocked from onlookers—that was his idea too.

"But what?" I urged, lifting my chin.

Jett held my gaze. "But before TJ tries getting you back…" He pulled away from the wall, stepped closer, and slid both hands onto my hips.

Holy smokes! They felt nice there. Warm and strong. A million parts of my body responded, like the entire system was going haywire.

Jett's gaze dropped to my lips. It was one of the telltale signs that a person wanted to kiss, and we both knew it. I could feel all the physical symptoms erupting inside me. Face warming. Heart pounding. I glanced at his lips in return. I couldn't help it. I wanted his kiss more than anything, and something about that fact scared and thrilled me all at once.

Jett lowered his head slowly, pausing once his mouth was a breath's space from mine. So close I could feel the warmth of his breath on my lips. I pulled in a heavenly breath and sighed. He must've just eaten a mint or something because the fresh scent was undeniable.

My eyes drifted shut just in time, and I tuned into the soft, testing touch of Jett's mouth on mine. Euphoria—a word used in one of the articles—poured over me.

I slid my hand up his broad shoulder and lifted my chin the slightest bit, causing our lips to touch once more. *So good. Unimaginably good.* I braced myself for more, knowing that Jett was just warming up.

He tightened his grip on my waist, tilted his head, and came in at last for a longer, more sensual kiss.

Yes. I tuned in to the gentle push and pull of his heavenly kiss as some sort of whimper echoed in my throat. Jett let out a raspy sigh of his own, igniting even more flames in my chest. *This* was how kissing was meant to feel, and I never wanted it to end.

Just as the thought ran through my mind, Jett slowed the kiss, pressed his lips to mine once more, then pulled away. He brushed his cheek against mine in the quiet space. "I've been dying to do that since junior high," he confessed in a whisper. His breath grazed my ear, making it very hard to pull out of the spell.

"You have?" I asked, shifting my focus to what he'd said.

"Of course." He'd said it like he was surprised I'd ever question it.

"Huh."

"Sure taking a long time to get those paints," a voice came from somewhere beyond the stage. I was pretty sure it was Connor.

Jett dropped his hands. "We better get back there."

I nodded. "Yeah. Why don't you go ahead? Tell them the paints weren't where I thought they'd be, so I'm checking another place."

He nodded, the mischief in his brown eyes making him look like an adorable—albeit guilty—child. "Good idea."

I bolted for the utility room when Jett spoke up once more. "Hey, Harper?"

I stopped short and spun on one heel. "What?"

He rushed back over to me and pressed his lips to mine once more, short, but oh, so sweet. A grin eased onto his face. "That's what." He disappeared behind the curtain.

I sat there staring into the black fabric folds as my limbs went weak. My legs like noodles, I leaned back against the wall and replayed the entire thing in my mind. From the incredible feel of his hands on my hips (*was that one in the chick magazines too?*) to the perfect way he led into the kiss. Slow and smooth and so so yummy.

TJ's last comment ran through my mind. *Have fun with Pastor Boy.*

I traced my fingers over my freshly kissed lips and grinned. *Don't worry, TJ. I will.* I wasn't exactly sure what was happening between me and Jett, but after a kiss like that I felt certain things would go someplace. Heck, maybe I'd even ask him to the Sadie's Hawkins dance.

It was then that I realized just what made that kiss better than it might have been had we kissed last night at the Burger Bar or at Jett's locker this morning—the absence of Tasha. I loved knowing that, though his ex-girlfriend was nowhere in sight, Jett still got me in some dark, wonderful place and kissed me. Kissed me in the most heavenly, dreamy way I could imagine.

With that happy realization putting a grin on my face, I hurried into the utility room, snatched the box of brushes and paints, and shuffled back through the narrow space as quickly as I could.

I'd barely made my way out of the heavy fabric folds when I heard someone speak up. "He doesn't actually like you."

I froze in place, my stomach dropping as I placed the voice in my head. I glanced over one shoulder to see that I was right—Tasha. She was hanging off the side of the ladder leading to the maintenance rafters.

"You didn't know we were watching, did you?"

I glanced up and spotted a few cheerleaders in uniform on the ledge.

"Yeah, well *Jett* knew. It's the only reason he kissed you.

Sorry to crush your dreams, but *I'm* the one he was thinking about."

A sharp knot of acknowledgment darted through the center of my chest.

I turned away from Tasha's green, glaring eyes and let the curtain fall behind me. Another horrific ache tore through me as I considered what Tasha had said. Suddenly it all made sense. He'd been doing it to get back at Tasha after all. I felt like an idiot. Not only did my newly ex-boyfriend like Tasha, it seemed Jett hadn't fully gotten over her.

I glanced over to Jett and the rest of our group where they sat hovered over posters on the floor. I had acted in several musical productions over the years, and I'd always been confident in my ability to play certain parts. But as I wandered back over to the group on the floor with the box, I realized I had nothing in my acting bag of tricks to make this right. Suddenly, I had no idea how to act around Jett.

CHAPTER NINE

"I thought Tasha was suspended from cheer," I griped before dunking my strawberry into a bowl of sour cream. Times like these called for a carpet picnic in the privacy of my room. Thank heavens Mom had gone on a fruit binge at the market.

"She *is* suspended," Summer said. "But that's not the same as kicked off the squad. She can't cheer at games or anything, but she still has to show up." Summer dropped a strawberry stem onto the tray and reached for another. "*And* she's not allowed to wear her uniform until the suspension is lifted."

I dabbed the tip of my strawberry into the brown sugar, rolling it until all the sour cream was coated, and paused before bringing it to my lips. "When we were researching the kiss," I started, "this article said that women were, like, instinctively drawn in by men whose immune systems carried what their own lacked, so their babies would have strong immune systems."

"That's cool," Bailey said. She was sitting up to my vanity rifling through my jewelry box and trying on my rings.

I replayed the effects of his kiss in my head and sighed. "I swear Jett and I would have kids with like, out of control immune systems. Probably superhero strength."

It took me a moment to realize that both Summer and Bailey were staring off in some sort of daze. "That good, huh?" Summer asked dreamily.

"*Indescribably* good," I assured. In fact, it was possible Jett had some super power of his own. "But I don't even know what to do now. What, are we in some dumb…let's-pretend-we-like-each-other-in-front-of-our-exes type of thing?"

Bailey gasped from her seat at my vanity and looked at me with wide eyes. "A fake relationship. Yes, I've seen that a million times. The couple starts out pretending like they're going out, all to make someone jealous or make a parent happy or something like that, but then they actually end up falling in love."

"Oh my heck, yes," Summer joined in. "That's perfect. If he's really just trying to make Tasha jealous, play along for now and it will turn into something more."

I hated how convinced they were that Jett was, in fact, just making Tasha jealous. Hated it because I was trying to convince myself otherwise. But what else did they have to go on? They hadn't seen the way Jett had flirted with me when Tasha wasn't there. Plus, I hadn't explained how very chivalrous he was when we were together. Although, he was probably just as chivalrous to random ladies at the store, being raised as he was.

"The idea that he was only kissing me to get back at Tasha…" It hurt to even say the words aloud. "That just ruins everything."

"I'm sure he likes you too," Bailey said. "I doubt he would've used just anyone."

"True. I hate the word *used* though. It's enough to make me just…wish I could forget about the whole thing."

"Yeah, but you still have to finish the assignment with him," Summer pointed out. "My vote is for you to jump into this whole fake relationship ruse with both feet. Ask him to the Sadie Hawkins dance even."

"Good idea," Bailey cheered. "Hurry and do it before Tasha does."

I gasped. "She would *never* do that. They're broken up. It would make her look desperate."

"Yeah, well TJ probably can't go since he's already graduated, and Tasha would never skip a dance."

I didn't volunteer the fact that TJ hadn't exactly received his diploma since he'd missed too much school. It was one of the things I'd been working on with him. Who knew what would happen with TJ's future now. Meanwhile, I wasn't even so sure Jett liked me the way I liked him. Which was bad.

If I thought I'd been crushing on Jett Bryant before all of this, now that he'd kissed me the way he had, I liked him so much it hurt.

I dropped the strawberry I was about to eat and

groaned. A hot and pounding sort of ruckus clanked around my heart. It felt like a pair of fists were tightening around the inside of my throat. "Just thinking about all of this is making me sick. I don't know why. I guess I'm just…"

"Afraid of rejection?" Summer guessed. "Worried about looking like an idiot? Scared that no matter what you do Jett will never feel the same?"

I shot her a glare. "Sheesh. Yes. All of the above, I guess."

"I know the perfect way to start playing the part," Bailey said with a clap. She hurried over to the goody tray and grabbed a big, lopsided strawberry. She wore a ring of mine on every finger including her thumbs. "You should go to his basketball games. They have a home game tonight."

Tonight's game wasn't exactly news to me since I'd overheard Connor and Jett talking about it. In fact, I could have sworn he hoped I was listening. Like he actually wanted me to show up.

If hope had a scale of zero to ten, mine moved from point-five to point-six. Maybe point-seven.

"Let's do it," Summer said.

The idea of seeing Jett Bryant in his element was definitely tempting.

I nodded. I might not agree to staging the whole fake romance idea like Summer and Bailey suggested, but I could go to his basketball game, couldn't I?

"Okay," I said with a nod.

A rush of new anticipation pushed through me as I

agreed, as if I'd somehow agreed to a whole lot more. I pushed back the odd dose of fear that came along with it. "Let's do it. Let's go to the game."

---

*S*omewhere in the back of my mind, I'd been entertaining what Summer and Bailey suggested. Tasha wasn't going to be able to cheer, but she *would* be at the game. And guess who else would probably be there? TJ.

And he was.

And so started the fake relationship ruse. That night I showed Tasha and TJ that Jett and I could play their little game too. Not only did I cheer from the bleachers as Jett played like a rockstar, I raced up to him after he'd tossed the winning basket during the last two seconds of the game. (Did I mention he plays like a rockstar?)

I locked eyes with Little Ms. Benched-from-the-Squad before propping myself onto my tiptoes and planting a kiss to his cheek. Sure, he had sweat dripping down just about every inch of his skin but the only word that came to me at the sight was *sexy*. A word that had *never* belonged to my vocabulary until that moment.

I kept this up on Monday by staying after school to watch Jett practice. This time was probably more convincing than me attending his game since TJ, of course, wasn't there and Tasha wasn't even in the gym. She was, however, on the grass beyond the window practicing cheers she wouldn't perform until her suspension was through.

As soon as Jett and I walked outside the double doors, he tossed his arm around me and pulled me close. He kissed the top of my head, which I thought was a cute addition, but I would have much preferred the kind of kiss he'd given me behind the curtain.

Then came Tuesday. In class that morning, Jett tapped my arm and leaned dangerously close to my ear. "Want to go to the Burger Bar tonight? It's supposed to be nice out. We can study in the back of my truck."

I had to rub my hands over the goosebumps he'd aroused on my arms before answering. "Yeah, that'd be good."

The problem was, I couldn't exactly tell if we were doing this to keep up the fake relationship ruse or because we had mutual feelings for one another. I knew where *I* stood, of course, but with Jett it wasn't so easy. Even as he told me he would pick me up at 6:00 that night, I realized that Levi was right there. Levi hung out with the MG's and was sure to get word back to Tasha.

Things like that kept me from knowing where Jett stood. Kept me from getting too excited about things between us. They also kept me wondering if I'd made a big mistake breaking things off with TJ, because who knew what his life was going to look like now? That's when I'd remind myself about the fact that TJ had locked lips with Tasha while we were together, which fueled my need to keep things up no matter what Jett's feelings were for me.

I couldn't help but think I needed to somehow put things to the test.

"The sooner you ask him to the dance, the better," Bailey said as we filed out of theater on Friday.

"I know," I mumbled, spotting the very Sadie's sign we made last week. "I'm thinking about it."

"Well, don't think too hard," Bailey warned. "I bet you anything that Tasha's going to ask him. And I heard that Pastor Bryant makes all his kids say *yes* to the first person who asks—no exceptions."

That *was* a frightening thought. One she hadn't shared with me before then. "Who told you that?" I asked.

Bailey dodged a group of guys shoving each other by the lockers. "Ava and Ivy Bryant are in my Spanish class," she explained.

"Huh." I pulled the theater binder to my chest, curled my fingers around the edges, and sighed.

I stared blankly toward the east hall, wondering if I'd see Jett there.

"Guess what else they told me," Bailey said. "With Jett being the captain and all, he got Coach to agree to early morning practices on Fridays instead, so the team gets their weekend nights free. Unless they have a game, that is."

An unwarranted thrill shot through my chest in a hot streak. "You're kidding."

Bailey popped her brows playfully. "Trying to free up his Fridays for you."

I hated that a grin came to my lips as I denied it. "I'm

not the reason he wants them free," I assured. Though I wished I was.

"Oh," Bailey suddenly blurted. "I told Summer I'd meet her in the back parking lot. Call me later?"

"Yeah, I'll call you." As I shuffled down the hallway, I thought back on my week with Jett. We hadn't shared an actual kiss since that incredible one last Friday. But on Tuesday night at the Burger Bar, we'd come very close to it.

We had scored wifi access long enough to pull up yet another article about kissing. Then, as I read the article aloud, Jett scooted closer to me, bringing his delicious smell and incredible warmth. He rested his forehead against mine and toyed with a lock of my hair, sending tingles to zip throughout my body. That alone had me feeling like my heart might stop. But then he added to the deliciousness of the moment by saying that he'd been dying to kiss me again. That he hadn't stopped thinking about that moment backstage.

I swear he was about to come in and prove that point when a startling horn blasted and jolted the two of us apart. I glared at the other side of the parking lot to find that—lo and behold—the offending honk had come from TJ's stupid truck. Tasha and her cronies had shown up after all. Dino and Jessie were piled into the flatbed with Olivia, Stacy, and the rest of the MG crew, while TJ and Tasha cozied up to one another in the front cab.

The mere recollection made me groan; the sound was swallowed up by the chaos in the hallway, squeaking shoes, slamming lockers, and distant conversations.

As I neared the end of the east hall, I glanced up from the array of high tops and fashion pumps to an entirely new sight. One that caused pleasure and pain to push through my body all at once. Jett Bryant—tall, dark, and proving to be dangerous for my health. He shot me a grin that revealed his dimple, which had me wondering if he was more a remedy instead.

Heaven help me.

"Hey," he said in that raspy voice.

I pulled my binder closer to my chest, dying to know if Tasha was nearby; her very presence had a way of discounting any exchange between me and Jett. "Hi."

He closed his locker and leaned against it, making everything else in that hallway a massive blur. It was the position he'd gotten into a moment before he kissed me. "Hey, I was going to ask about this whole rule your mom had about seeing a different guy between dates and all that."

My insides were trying to throw a celebration parade at his question, but I told them to quiet down and not read too much into things yet. "Well, she changed the rule a little bit, since she doesn't want me to start seeing TJ again."

Jett lifted his brow. "Smart woman. Remind me to bring her a rose next time I come out."

That statement was like a rolling drumbeat for the parade threatening to march within me. Mainly because we'd officially put in all twelve of our study hours. In fact, we'd finished the assignment just last night and handed it in this morning.

"So now the rule is that if I want to date just one guy that's fine, but I can't, like, see him two nights in a row. Except if I'm going to your games or your practices since that doesn't exactly count as a date."

He held my gaze for a moment before taking a step forward. He was now leaning on someone else's locker but that didn't seem to bother him. "What about if we study one night, whatever homework we have, and go out the next? Would she be okay with that?"

His question made it seem very much like he was asking me out for tonight since we'd been studying together the night before. The parade officially started its march. "I think so. I mean, yeah, for sure she would." And if she didn't, I'd sneak out. Or at least that's what the marching band was suggesting.

"So let's go someplace tonight. Just me and you," he said, voice low and raspy.

I cleared my throat. "Okay. That sounds fun."

He held my gaze once more, an almost puzzled expression pulling at his handsome brow. Was he trying to figure it out too? Perhaps he was just as confused as I was. I hoped so.

"Great," he finally said. "Pick you up at seven?"

I nodded, ready to take up my cymbals and join in the march. "Perfect."

CHAPTER TEN

When Jett picked me up, he actually did bring my mom a rose. Mom loved the gesture, and when she told him as much, Jett shot me a sly wink to remind me of our conversation earlier. I hadn't forgotten.

Missy, who practically lived in her tutu now, showed off a few moves for him while my mom put the rose in water. My favorite part of that moment was when Jett told Missy to take his hand so he could spin her around. She did, and to say that my heart melted a little would be an understatement. I'm pretty sure the entire organ turned to a pile of pulsing goo in my chest. Jett was really starting to seem like the full package.

"You brought your appetite, right?" Jett asked once he was settled behind the wheel of his truck.

I glanced at the sack of groceries on the seat between us and nodded. "Yep."

"Good." He grinned and roared up the engine.

I noticed two ATV's in the flatbed as Jett walked me to his truck. Something else that hadn't escaped my attention was Jett's letterman jacket draped along the back of the middle seat. I'd returned it earlier that week, but something told me he'd brought it just for me. It seemed he had plans for us to be outside, and evenings were really starting to cool down in Sweet Water.

"So I know I mentioned in the hallway that it'd be just the two of us," Jett started.

I glanced over, preparing myself for the worst. "Uh huh," I urged. Great. What would he say now? That our exes were going to be doubling with us?

"Ava and Ivy wanted to take the ATV's on the beach tonight with Connor and Levi, so I thought it might be fun if we joined them. Kind of like a big group date."

I liked the sound of that. Getting to know his family a bit more. "I'd love that." His twin sisters were ridiculously beautiful but their outright kindness to everyone in sight made it impossible to hate them for it.

"Good." Jett stretched an arm over the groceries and rested his hand, palm up, on my lap.

It took a fraction of a second to realize he wanted to hold my hand. I gulped, paced my frantic, fluttering breath, then slid my palm into his. Jett curled his fingers around mine, tightening his grip, and shot me that smile that threatened to make my breath hitch. "Might be a good time to tell you—since my sisters will be there and all—that my parents are sort of separated right now."

Wow. I couldn't believe he'd actually opened up to me about it. "I'm sorry," I said softly.

He shrugged. "Pastor's family's supposed to be perfect, right? So I guess it feels a little…hard to talk about. My dad doesn't want to make the congregation panic or anything."

I nodded, wrapped my other hand around the back of his, and relished in the connection for a moment. It felt very…boyfriend and girlfriend-ish. "Yeah, that makes sense. Do you think they'll be able to work through it?"

Jett shook his head, slowing as we came upon a roundabout. "It's hard to say. I think…I mean, maybe I'm just naïve, but I can't actually picture them ever *not* together. The whole thing kind of freaks me out, really. The twins, too. We don't know what to think about it."

I nodded, not wanting him to feel like he had to share more. I mainly just wanted to be someone he could confide in. I liked knowing that, in a way, I was.

As we drove to the beach, I traced the tips of my fingers up Jett's wrist and along the inside of his arm. I moved to the outer part of his bicep next, tracing back down in a slow trickle, hoping it would soothe the upset in his heart over his parents. When I was younger, I hated thinking about my parents splitting up. I realized it was probably no easier at our age.

"You know," I said, looking over the glistening water as we headed toward the parking area. The sun was starting to set, and the sight was stunning. An array of red, gold, and every shade in between stretched all the way to the water, where it reflected over the waves. "I used to think that I might be able to keep my parents together somehow. I turned ten about a month before my dad left. My mom was pregnant with Missy at the time."

A knot of pain seeped into my chest at the recollection. Knowing that Jett was possibly facing a similar thing made the wounds feel fresh. "I remember thinking that I must be a real disappointment or something, because it was like, as soon as he found out they were having another girl—not a boy—he took off." I released a dark chuckle under my breath. "It was literally the day after the ultrasound." I shrugged and cupped both of my hands around his once more. "It's probably for the best. What good would it have done for him to stick around longer just because he was excited about finally getting a boy? It wouldn't have changed him."

The pain of that truth was like a dozen darts to the chest. I hadn't even admitted it to myself before that moment. But I was suddenly very sick of giving my dad excuses. Giving into every *what-if* scenario I could imagine.

Jett squeezed my hand. "You're probably right," he said softly. "It's really odd, but with my mom, she isn't going wild or anything. She's just...I don't know. I looked it up, and read that a lot of people, before they hit some milestone age, get a little...*off*. She's about to turn forty later this year, and I wonder if she regrets getting married so young. She had me when she was twenty-one."

I chuckled. "My mom was nineteen when I came along."

Jett grinned. "Both were young. Like I said, my folks

haven't given us a lot of details. Originally, she went to Georgia to help my grandma get through a couple of back-to-back surgeries. She needed help getting around and stuff. That was back when school started."

Jett squinted as he slowed the truck and pulled into the parking area. He turned the key to shut off the engine, moved the sack of groceries onto the floor, and scooted closer to me in the small space.

"After the surgeries were through, my mom just kind of stayed out there. She came back for my birthday last month, but instead of settling back in, she gathered a few *more* of her things. Sweaters, jackets, winter-type clothes. That's when they told us she was staying out there for more than my grandma. My dad says she needs space and time to work through a few things. She basically says the same thing."

I sighed, wishing I could give him some sort of assurance. The truth was, I had nothing. Except... "You guys will be fine either way," I said. "I mean, it's awful, and I really hope they don't split up, but I've realized that people are pretty resilient."

"*You* definitely are." Jett swept a strand of my hair behind my ear and let his fingers trace along the side of my neck.

The sensation caused goosebumps to ripple over my arms. My heart kicked up a beat.

"You've been through a lot, Harper. You really have. And you've always seemed so...I don't know, cheerful." He laughed. "Is that a dumb word?"

I shook my head and grinned, suddenly fighting back

an onslaught of emotion. "No. I like that word. And I'm glad. I *have* been a pretty happy kid, all things considered. My mom's amazing. She never wanted us to feel like we were missing anything, you know? In fact, her parents moved out here after he left. They come over a lot, which has really helped. They're awesome."

I stared into Jett's heavenly brown eyes, my heart swelling as I detected emotion there as well. "I want Missy to have the best life ever," I said in a whisper. "My mom too. She deserves it."

Jett ran his thumb along my cheek, his gaze still locked on me. "You deserve that too." He moved in then, brushed his lips gently to mine, and kissed me in the most tender, beautiful way. It felt like more than an outward connection of his mouth on mine; it was like our souls were entwined. Soothing and encouraging one another in a moment more intimate than anything I'd known.

He kissed me again, long and slow, as the tone shifted into something more sensual. I tilted my head, ran my hand up the back of his neck, and deepened the kiss with a sigh. *So good.* Even better than I remembered. I keyed in to every sensation: the movement of his masterful lips, strong and persuasive one moment, gentle and caressing the next. And when he ever so softly grazed my tongue with his, hints of hot cinnamon candy made things all the sweeter.

I wasn't sure how much time ticked on as we kissed in Jett's truck. All I knew was that the moment bonded us to one another in a way that I couldn't explain. Jett wasn't like a lot of other guys out there, looking for cheap thrills with random girls, all to use them one day and dump them the next. I secretly thrilled in how very different he was from TJ. Jett was driven and determined. He wanted to find someone he could share a future with. Have a family with. He wanted what I wanted, and I never realized how attractive that quality was.

But the very best part was that nobody was in sight. It was *our* time—mine and Jett's alone—which told me everything I needed to know: Jett really was interested in me, the way I was in him.

With that welcome truth flowing through me, I tuned into the wonder of Jett's lips on mine—the chemistry of *our* kiss—determined to never let go of him.

A series of taps echoed throughout the cab suddenly, ripping me from my musings in one startling blink.

Jett pulled back with a groan and glared at the window behind me. "Great," he mumbled under his breath. "They're here."

They. They. Please say *they* didn't mean TJ and Tasha. Panic trampled over the peace of the moment, reminding me that perhaps this wasn't as real as I hoped it might be.

Heart thudding out its frantic beat, I glanced over my shoulder to see Connor, Levi, and Jett's twin sisters huddled up to the window.

"Excuse me," Connor said while cupping a fist over his mouth. It made it sound like he was speaking through a megaphone. "We're going to need you to release the girl and step out of your vehicle with your hands up."

Ava gave Connor a playful slap. "You're such a dork."

Thankfully, the group moved to the back of the truck

to help unload the ATV's, allowing me and Jett a chance to climb out of the truck without an audience. I was grateful for that. After helping me down, Jett snatched his jacket off the seat.

He lifted a brow. "You want?"

I grinned. "Yes, thank you." I slid my arms into place as he held it up for me and offered to carry the groceries so he could help with the ATV's. And soon I was huddled beside Ava and Ivy, watching as the guys placed boards as ramps to lower the 4-wheelers.

"This is going to be a blast," Ava cheered with a grin.

"Totally," I agreed.

Ivy scrunched her face up as she watched Levi roar one of the ATV's to life. "*If* they can get them down from the truck in one piece."

The three of us laughed. "Right," I said. But inwardly, I was just realizing something. Levi was friends with a lot of the mean girls. Could it be that Jett had seen them coming and purposely kissed me at that moment?

No, Harper, I scolded myself. What we shared was real, I was sure of it. I swallowed the intrusive doubts in my head and tightened my grip on the bag of groceries. I had all the assurance I needed. Tomorrow I'd ask Jett to the dance, just like I planned. If our relationship had started off as some sort of sham, it had quickly evolved into something more. This was definitely the real thing. I'd keep that thought at the front of my mind, and block out the rest.

CHAPTER ELEVEN

"So, what do you think?" I asked as I stared at the poster before us. A dozen photos of Jett and I were pasted along the bottom half. Pictures that had been taken just last night at the beach. Some were selfies, but others were shot by Ava who, according to Jett, had her mother's flare for photography. She'd forwarded them to Jett who forwarded them to me, which gave me the idea to ask *this* way instead of the way I'd planned prior.

"I think it's the most adorable thing I've ever seen," Summer said in an almost reverent tone. "You guys look perfect together."

"Agreed," Bailey said with a sigh.

I moved my gaze from the prints of us by last night's campfire, cuddled up to each other on the ATV, and the one of Jett lifting me in his arms (my favorite) to the question I'd poised in colorful markers above it: *Can you "picture" us at the Sadie Hawkins dance together?*

"You guys are seriously the cutest couple ever," Summer said.

I glanced down at the ring I was spinning around my finger. Jett had given it to me last night. He'd pointed out the charms attached to many of the rings I'd worn, which made the charm on this one just perfect: a set of smooching lips. *"So you'll never forget the time we learned about the chemistry of a kiss."*

My heart melted at the very recollection. Forget? Impossible. Of all the rings I'd gotten over the years, this would forever be my favorite, I was sure of it.

Jett was busy putting in his double shift for the day, like he did most Saturdays, while his dad and the twins met Jett's mom for lunch someplace between Atlanta and Sweet Water. That meant we could set up the poster, the candy, and the basketball balloons I got him whenever we wanted. I decided since Jett's shift ended at seven that night, we'd drop it off around six-thirty and have it waiting there for him when he pulled into the driveway.

I hoped that one week was enough notice. The dance was on Saturday, after all.

A mountain of nerves built inside me as I pulled into Jett's cul-de-sac. No cars or trucks sat parked beyond the garage. And when I took a peek inside, I saw that the garage was empty as well. *Perfect.* In about thirty minutes, Jett would drive up and see what was on the porch. Part of me wished I could be there to witness it.

We worked quickly, propping the poster with two big rocks. I used those same rocks to weigh down the helium balloons I'd bought to go with it. We sprinkled the porch with chocolate kisses and cinnamon candies (the combination stealthily symbolizing our hot kisses) and stepped back to check out our work.

"It's perfect," Bailey said with a nod.

"Totally," Summer agreed.

I thought so too. For a brief moment, I considered snapping a picture of the display, but I thought better of it. Ava would probably do that. Maybe she'd make him pose in front of it as well—that would be so cute!

I grinned. "All right, I guess we're good." Anticipation fluttered through me as I pictured Jett walking onto the scene. I nodded, enjoying the burst of warmth that image brought, and forced my eyes off the sight. "Guess we better take off before he gets here."

I couldn't help but think, as we hurried back to the car, that Jett and I were stepping into new territory. Dates that didn't revolve around our exes and what they had planned. We were on our very own journey, as a new couple, and I couldn't wait to see where it led.

CHAPTER TWELVE

I really wanted Jett to hurry and answer back, but I was a senior now and I knew how this worked: Jett could answer how and when he wanted, and it was my job (as the one who asked) to smile, wait, and not mention the dance invite until he did.

Besides, it usually took at least a few days (sometimes longer) because guys wanted to think of a clever way to respond, often incorporating the same theme.

I reminded myself of that very thing when Sunday went by without an answer. Part of me was hoping he'd put me out of my misery by bringing it up at Sunday service. You know, say something like, *"I found the most awesome thing on my porch when I came home from work last night."* Or *"Wish I could think of a good way to answer this hot girl who asked me to the dance."*

But he gave me no such thing.

On Monday in class, he said something a little

encouraging after bumping my elbow to gain my attention. "I got Saturday off work," he said under his breath.

I yanked my eyes off Ms. Tolken and her polyester suit to catch his gaze. Was he about to say *yes* right here and now? I would welcome the idea with open arms. He didn't have to answer in some special way; he just needed to answer.

He shrugged and added, "Just so you know."

Just so you know? "That's awesome," I said with an encouraging nod.

But, as Mr. Meadows would say, encourage him it did not. Jett said nothing more of it. In fact, he told me after school ended that practice would run late and he had an essay to write. "I'll text you later," he'd promised, but that did little to assure me, and if I were being honest, he seemed a little…off.

I climbed into bed early that night, feeling very determined to stay focused on positive thoughts. Maybe Jett was distancing himself a little so he could surprise me by answering in some fun way. Yes, that made perfect sense. Things were good.

My phone buzzed with a text just then, and the fact that it was from Jett seemed to prove my point.

Just got back from practice. Gonna crank out this essay now. I missed hanging out today. You free tomorrow night?

The worst part about this text was the fact that I was *not* free. Mom had made dinner plans with my grandparents before they took off on their month-long vacation to Florida. I'd already begged her to let Jett come along but she said no, insisting that I'd ignore everyone but Jett the entire time. She went on to assure me that we could include him in things like that if we were still dating when her parents got back from Florida.

I stared at my phone for ten solid minutes, wishing there was a way around this whole dinner party. Thoughts of faking sick came to mind, but guilt about not saying goodbye to my grandparents squashed that idea. So I finally relented.

I missed hanging out with you too. I've got to do dinner with the grandparents tomorrow night. Maybe after I get back if it's not too late?

I had to add that part. The truth was, I'd sneak him right into my room that night if I had to. I just wanted to…to make sure I was only imagining Jett's distant manner.

I stared at the screen, waiting for his response, hoping he'd say that sounded good. When no reply came, I hopped onto social media and scrolled through dozens of posts about couples going to Sadies. I hoped Jett would hurry and answer me so I could write one of those *he said yes* posts as well.

My phone buzzed then, and I swiped over to read his text.

Yeah, that'd be good. I forgot to tell you. Coach says we have to bring our letterman jackets for the assembly tomorrow. Would you mind bringing it?

I clenched my eyes against the sentence, willing it to not penetrate the shield I'd built, but it was already too late. He hadn't said yes to the dance yet, he hadn't hung out with me tonight (something he usually tried to do no matter the circumstance), and now he wanted his jacket back. These were signs, weren't they?

My heart felt like it was growing knots. A dozen of them with sharp and prickly points.

I thought back on our time in his truck Friday night. The intimate moments we'd shared. Had they meant more to me than they had Jett? What if he'd only wanted to use me all along so he could get Tasha back? I tried very hard to reject that idea by reminding myself of the moments we shared when no one else was there.

But what if he *had* only been faking all along? It would make sense for him to panic and pull away once I asked him to the dance. Unless he wanted to use it as a way to make Tasha jealous even still. If that really *was* his incentive, he'd feel bad if he thought I was starting to fall for him. The guy had a conscience, I knew that much.

But then a very ugly thought hit my mind like a train: What if he was waiting for a better offer? Better, as in, from Tasha?

My stomach clenched at the thought.

Come on, Harper. It's been two days for crying out loud. Give the guy a minute to reply.

But it was more than just his lack of reply that had me in knots. When you add on his distant manner and now the whole jacket thing…

This was my punishment for not helping TJ the way I was meant to. I knew it. I was being selfish by pursuing a man who'd be perfectly healthy with or without me. I should…what, sacrifice my own happiness at the *off* chance I could make a difference?

I rolled my eyes at how stupid I sounded. And had I forgotten about the fact that TJ picked Tasha over me by making out with her while we were dating?

"Right," I muttered to myself.

I felt proud for not letting guilt about TJ bring me to an even lower state. It didn't take care of my problem with Jett, but at least it didn't add to it. I realized then that I hadn't replied to Jett about the jacket. I readied my thumbs, stared at the screen, and wondered if I should just be upfront with him about the dance. Why was I tiptoeing around the issue? So what if it was taboo to talk about until the answer came. The answer *hadn't* come and I only had a few days left to plan.

Okay, so what would I say to him? I tried tapping it out as an idea came to mind. *So I know this is kind of awkward…* "Oh my gosh, no!" I held a heavy thumb on the delete button until the stupid sentence disappeared.

The cursor was still flashing at me so I tried again. *Bailey and Summer were talking about going on a big group date for Saturday. I know you haven't answered me back yet, but…* "No, that's ridiculous." I put my thumb into action again, tapping triple time on the delete button.

I'd just have to do it in person. I would. I'd do it first thing in the morning. With my determination set, I tapped out a new reply.

Yeah, I'll bring your jacket. Night.

I hit send and groaned. "There. You happy?" I snapped to Jett through my phone.

A text popped up in reply. *Thanks. Night, Harper. Sweet dreams.*

I shook my head and plopped my phone back onto the nightstand. I had no idea what was going on between us, and his texts were only making things worse. Sweet dreams, huh? I was pretty sure I was in for anything but.

CHAPTER THIRTEEN

I entered the school through the east hallway with Jett on my mind. We hadn't kissed since Friday night and I was beginning to go through withdrawal. A very large part of me wanted to march up to him, back him up against the locker, and remind him of what we'd shared in his truck last week.

In case he'd forgotten over the last few days. Meanwhile I was over here replaying the scene in my mind (with great detail, I might add) a hundred times a day.

Despite the fact that it was chilly out, I opted to *not* wear Jett's jacket. It would just feel too shameful to shrug out of it before handing it back. It was bad enough that I had to let go of it at all. But I was starting to believe that I didn't deserve to have a boyfriend so good; that I was destined to latch myself only to men who needed to be rescued from themselves—not that I'd be able to do anything about it.

I had seriously considered staying home for the day and letting Summer or Bailey bring his jacket to him, but my curiosity about the assembly won out. Plus, I really couldn't go around missing school without being punished for it later. If not by my mom, then by the sheer amount of makeup work.

And then there was the small vow I'd made yesterday to confront him about the dance. I *had* to do that today no matter how awkward it felt.

Sadly, Jett was nowhere to be found. In fact, I scanned the adjacent lockers where a bunch of his teammates usually stood, but didn't find any of the guys there either. Suddenly, I heard the frantic call of my name.

"Harper, we need his jacket."

I looked over to see Tasha weaving her way past a group of sophomores. Her bright green eyes were focused on the jacket draped over my arm. She held her hand out as she neared and added, "Okay?"

But it wasn't. It was *not* okay that I was supposed to hand Jett's letterman jacket over to his vicious ex-girlfriend without a care in the world.

Heat boiled up the back of my shoulders and neck. I glanced down at the name and number stitched on the front, hating the idea of Tasha prancing along the hall while it hung loosely off her shoulders.

"Where *is* Jett?" I asked.

"Practicing for the assembly, of course." She thrust her

hand toward me once more. "C'mon, I've really got to get back in there."

The fact that she was dressed in uniform said that her probation period was over and she was probably in the assembly with him, which made sense. The cheerleaders were almost always part of the assemblies.

"Here," I finally said, forcing myself to hand it over.

Tasha snatched it with a fast fist. "Thanks." She shot me a smug-looking grin and tipped her head to one side. "You coming to the assembly?"

Nausea worked its way through my gut in a cold, slow crawl. "I'm not sure," I said. The last thing I wanted was to give Tasha the satisfaction of being part of her adoring audience.

She gasped theatrically. "Why not? Jett will be in it, and you're, like, claiming that he's your boyfriend now, aren't you?"

I gulped. "I'm not *claiming* anything."

She held my gaze for a moment more, then nodded. "Too bad he can't really get over me, isn't it? If I wanted, I could have Jett back like *this.*" She snapped her fingers in front of my face.

I flinched, but the fury fuse had been lit and there was no stopping the response it triggered. "Wow," I blurted. "One minute you want TJ, the next you want Jett back. Make up your mind, Tasha. It seems like you want whoever *I'm* with." I did a theatrical move of my own—a head tilt as I placed a finger beneath my chin in wonder. "Tell me, are we in some sort of competition, because I think I missed the memo?"

"This coming from the girl who used to chase *my* boyfriend down and kiss him on the playground."

The angry heat spread like wildfire to my chest. "Get over it, Tasha. How many kindergarten memories are you clinging to?"

"Break it up, girls," came a familiar voice. I glanced over to see Connor standing nearby. Levi was there too, a concerned expression on his face.

In fact, a small crowd had gathered around us. I looked beyond Jett's friends, hoping to see Jett there for myself, but failing.

"I'll take that," Levi said. He snatched the jacket out of her hand and took off back down the hall.

I hid a satisfied grin; at least Tasha wouldn't be wearing it.

"Let's go, Tasha," Connor said.

The pint-sized brunette shot me a squinty-eyed glare and waved at me with flittering fingers. "Bah-bye, now."

I caught Connor giving me a lingering look after Tasha left. "Sorry," he said when our eyes met. "She's a brat."

I shrugged, hoping it would make up for the heat I felt pooling into my face. "I can take it."

Connor looked down the hallway then back to me, his weight shifting from one foot to the next. "I, um… everything okay with you and Jett?"

"What?" The bell rang out, blasting over my response. "What do you mean?"

"Crap," he mumbled while glancing at his watch. "I've got to go. I'll…we'll talk later." He darted around the crowd as lockers slammed and students made their way to class.

Holy *Adrenalineville.* My heart was going all sorts of crazy. I was mad and embarrassed all at once. Add a mass of confusion to that after Connor's question, and you have one hot disaster.

"They don't call them the Mean Girls for nothing," one girl said to me as she closed a nearby locker—a pretty blonde I'd seen around school but never spoken to.

"Yeah." I forced a smile. "I guess you're right."

I made my way to first period in a daze, asking myself if I could handle the dumb assembly. While Ms. Tolken took roll, I drew up a pie chart depicting my ability to handle whatever might happen with Jett in front of the entire school. And why had Tasha acted so surprised when I said I might not go? Connor had asked if I was angry with Jett next…

I asked him to the dance, hadn't I? Did he think I was mad at Jett for not answering yet? An idea came very close to my mind, but it flittered off as I tried to catch hold of it.

Something about the dance and the fact that Jett hadn't answered me—*that was it!* He was going to answer me during the assembly, wasn't he?

The anger clenching my arms and back gave way to a new sense of elation.

"Time to head on down to the assembly," Ms. Tolken announced. She removed the dark-rimmed glasses, revealing a face that could possibly belong to a super model, and squared a warning look over the class. "If you get caught trying to sneak off and step out during the assembly, you *will* be marked truant."

Oh, there was no worry about that. Not anymore. This time I nearly floated down that hallway, carried by thoughts of Jett Bryant telling me *yes* in front of the entire school. I loved the idea. I loved it so much that I didn't even care if Tasha wanted to flatter herself and say it was all some act to make her jealous. I knew better, and that's all that mattered.

The drill team started things off with a song by Nirvana to get everyone hyped up about the Sadie Hawkins dance. It worked. By the time Coach came out to explain why we should be exceptionally proud of both our boys and girls basketball teams the gymnasium was in a state of chaos, cheering wildly after every word he said.

When he introduced the captain of the boys team, Mr. Brown Eyes himself, the school exploded. The captain of the girls team roused a similar response, and soon both captains—along with their co-captains—lined up along the front and slipped on a pair of sunglasses.

A new song kicked up with a heavy beat, this one by INXS. Suddenly the rest of the teams danced onto the court, the guys from one side, the girls from the other. Just when I thought they'd leave it at that and filter off the court, the song changed and the cheerleaders entered the scene in an array of acrobatic moves.

I tore my eyes off Jett and all of his masculine glory to check for Tasha. It'd be just like her to pair up with him somehow. Lo and behold, she was there, and shimmying her way right over to Jett. I watched in horror as four cheerleaders paired up with the captains and co-captains, male cheerleaders for the girls, female ones for the boys.

A small ache stabbed right into my chest as Jett took Tasha by the waist and lifted her off the ground in a dance move that went right to the beat. Was this the *practice* he'd stayed after for last night?

Tasha spun around then, and Jett moved down to one knee in time for Tasha to sit on his other leg and toss her arm around the back of his neck. The exact move was played out with the others as well but all I could focus on was Jett.

The song ended at last and everyone else in the gymnasium burst into applause. I began a countdown in my head, wondering how long it would take for Tasha to get her grubs off of Jett.

"I've been waiting until today to answer you," came a voice from the mic over the crowd. It took me a moment to locate Kenny, another guy from the team. He stood up front, shifting his weight from one foot to the next while twisting the cord around his finger. A hush fell over the crowd. "Annie Chetler, where are you?"

A round of squeals sounded from one section of the bleachers, and a petite blonde girl came to a stand. The one from the hall, I realized.

"Come on down here, and you'll get your answer," Kenny said, twiddling the cord some more.

A couple of the male cheerleaders made a bench for her out of their legs where Annie took a seat and watched Kenny bust into a few dance moves with a cheerleader on either side of him. At last they spun away from her, produced some cards they'd had tucked out of sight, and spun back to reveal the letters *YES*.

This time I joined in on the cheering. My heart joined in too, beating double time as I saw exactly what I'd hoped might happen becoming a very real probability. I'd forgive him for waiting so long if he'd done it to simply answer me during the assembly.

I watched two other guys answer two other girls, one of whom was on the girls basketball team. I glanced over to see if Jett would move up to the microphone between each one, but so far he'd stayed tucked into a cluster by his teammates where they watched the action.

I wasn't sure where Tasha had gone off to, but she made her reappearance by stepping up to the microphone. While grabbing it with one hand, she cheered with the other by pumping a fist and thrusting it high over her head.

"J, E, T, T, will you go to the dance with me?"

The rest of the cheer team gathered around her and repeated the phrase while my brain tried to process what I'd just heard.

"J, E, T, T, will you go to the dance with me?"

Wait a minute, *Tasha* was asking *Jett* to Sadie's?

Tasha took the lead again. "I know it's late but we both need a date, so what's it gonna be?"

The squad echoed that line as well while Tasha urged Jett front and center with a curling finger.

Nausea roared through me like a wild beast. I wanted to throw up and punch something all at the same time.

Jett shuffled casually to the appointed spot and glanced

up and over the bleachers. I got the impression that he was looking for me. Did he know how furious I was? How hurt and confused and angry I was that he hadn't just answered me? None of this would be happening right now if he had just told me yes.

But perhaps that was just it. Maybe this is what he'd been wanting all along. To make Tasha jealous enough to come crawling back. At least this way, he might not look so pathetic for taking her back. After all, who could turn someone down in front of the entire school?

Tasha danced a circle around Jett, twirling a finger on his shoulders and sang out one more line. "Check your pockets and you will find one of the answers you have in mind. Yes or no, what will it be? Please hold it up for me to see."

A hush fell over the crowd once more.

A drumbeat picked up as Jett shoved his hands into his pockets.

"Say yes," a random guy shouted from the bleachers. A few students chuckled.

Jett tugged a card from each pocket and proceeded to open both. He stared at them for a bit, then shot a look at me exactly where I sat. My heart stopped. I was sure of it, as one side of his lip quirked up. It looked more like an apology than a grin.

I gulped, and it felt like acid had snuck up my throat.

At last he shoved one of the cards back into his pocket and turned the sign so it faced the crowd and Tasha, who'd backed away from him so everyone could see.

Y. E. S. The bright red letters had matching lip blotches around them, and the sight felt like eyeball stabs.

The school erupted in the loudest, echoing cheer of the entire event. Tasha bolted over, grabbed hold of his wrist and raised his hand triumphantly over his head, rousing an even bigger response.

That was it. I'd had all I could handle. More than I could take, in fact. I shuffled my way off the bleachers in a rush, wishing more than anything I could be invisible until I got to my car. I wasn't sure where I was going or what I planned to do. I only knew I had to get out of there, and quick.

Bailey and Summer, who'd been helping with the sound system for the assembly, must have abandoned the scene too because I heard them calling after me down the hall.

"Harper, wait!"

But there was no way. The tears were about to win out and I couldn't let that happen until I was alone. So I kept running over the squeaky floors, pretending not to hear my friends, and pushed my way through the double doors at the end of the hall.

Tears blurred my vision once I hit the lot, complicating my hurried path as I weaved through one cluster of cars after the next until I came to my Jetta.

I climbed in quickly, closed the door behind me, and gripped the steering wheel with numb fingers. A streak of sunlight shone on the track in the distance, highlighting a set of javelins against the fence. I cringed, feeling as if a javelin the size of Sweet Water was ripping its way through my chest. The burning ache made it hard to catch my next breath. I clenched my eyes against the pain, willing myself to wipe up the tears and drive my butt as far away from Jett as I could get.

Lord, how could I have been so wrong?

Another flaming javelin came ripping through.

My phone buzzed with a text, and then another. Of course I hoped they were from Jett, though I'm sure he was too busy falling all over Tasha while everyone congratulated them about getting back together. I wasn't even sure they *were* back together. Maybe he just said yes because he didn't dare to say no in front of everyone. Or maybe I was in denial.

A quick glance at my screen said the texts were from a group chat between me, Bailey, and Summer.

Bailey's came first. *Jett is a total jerk for doing that. Do you want us to come with you while you confront him?*

Summer's came next. *Come back and talk to him. This doesn't seem like something Jett would do.*

She was right, but he'd done it. The entire school had witnessed it. And the thing was, all of this was at least partially my fault. I'd been willing to take part in some ruse. One to make our exes jealous. And now Jett had gotten what he really wanted out of it. Turns out, that wasn't me.

My chest burned with hot, achy breaths as I tapped out a quick reply.

Please, whatever you do, don't say anything to him or his friends. I think I know why he did this, and I want to talk to him about it myself.

I hit send, shoved my key into the ignition, and roared up the engine. I had zero intention of actually confronting Jett, but I didn't feel bad for lying about it either. I'd said the one thing that would stop Bailey and Summer from trying to fix this for me.

Jett wanted his ex back, and he'd used the one girl who'd always wanted him to do it. Nothing anyone said or did could fix that. With that horrid truth in my mind, I headed toward home.

CHAPTER FOURTEEN

I tried to get out of dinner with the grandparents that night but when my mom and Missy told them that I wasn't coming, Gramps moseyed right on into my room, sat at the foot of my bed, and tapped the covers I was hiding under.

"Knock knock, Gal," he said in that raspy voice of his.

"Who's there?" I asked, my lips grazing the drooping sheet.

"Iffy," he grumbled.

I might have been gripped by more layers of devastation than I'd known in all my seventeen years, but I had to know where he was going with this. "Iffy who?"

"If ye don't come to dinner with us tonight, you'll make ye grandma and I cry."

I clenched my eyes shut under the covers and stifled a groan. How in the world could I say no to that? My mom was always reminding me that we didn't know how long they'd be with us; I didn't want to regret this moment for the rest of my life.

All the way to the restaurant, I imagined sitting at the table with my family, checking out the menu, and placing my order for all to hear. *"I'll take three pints of ice cream with a jumbo spoon, one box of tissues—could you make those extra soft? And a paper bag to hide under while I bawl my face off."*

I felt so sad and miserable and...humiliated! Just moments before the horrible incident, I'd convinced myself that Jett would be answering *me* with a giant YES at the assembly. I assumed he would call or text once the assembly was through, but he had the nerve to wait until school was over, which I thought was ridiculous and insulting and showed just how immature he actually was. And here I'd thought he was better than TJ all this time. *Huh!*

I waited clear until dinner was through to pull out my phone and reread the text he'd sent me. *Have fun with your grandparents tonight. Maybe I could swing by once you guys are through?*

I hadn't answered him back yet because I wasn't sure what kind of stupid game he was playing. I'd expected him to at least *acknowledge* the fact that I. Asked. Him. First! What did he want to say now? *"Hope you and I were on the same page. You wanted TJ and I wanted Tasha, right?"* And even if that *wasn't* the case, even if Jett really did like me, what sort of excuse could he possibly have for ignoring my invite while saying yes to hers?

Back at home Gramps patted my back and planted a kiss to the top of my head. "Night, Gal. You stay away from those boys now, ya hear? They're nothing but trouble."

Grams chuckled and gave his cheeks a pat. "I ought to know." She moved in, and the two sandwiched me in a hug. Floral perfume mingled with Old Spice as I wrapped my arms around them in return, fighting the moisture threatening to spill from my eyes.

"You don't need to worry about the boys," my mom said. "Harper's dating the pastor's son."

Was I, though?

Missy danced a circle around us in the entryway. "Yeah, and he's *cute,*" she squealed with a clap.

Grams chuckled. "Uh oh, better watch out. She's already boy crazy." Grams moved over to give Missy a hug next, but Gramps stayed at my side.

"You know us guys aren't the smartest creatures," he mumbled under his breath. "Don't be afraid to give that fellow of yours a little...*guidance,* if you know what I mean."

"A *lot* of guidance," Grams blurted, proving that her hearing aids were in top form. "If I hadn't told this guy exactly what I needed over the years, we'd have both gone crazy."

I laughed, but inside I was practically tripping over Grams' comment. Gramps was like, the perfect husband. Always attentive. Helping her with her coat. Asking the waiter to refill her glass or bring an extra pat of butter so she didn't have to do it herself.

I considered that long after we'd said goodnight to the happiest couple I knew. Why had Gramps said that? Had he sensed something was wrong? I couldn't help but roll my eyes at myself as I recalled the way he'd knocked on the covers over my head and guilted me into going to dinner. Of *course* he knew something was wrong. I'd been moping the entire night.

"Harper, were you going to get that outlet replaced in my bathroom?" Mom asked from the top of the stairs. "I really don't want to curl my hair in the kid's bathroom again."

Sounds of a bath running for Missy echoed down the stairs as she darted across the hall in a towel. "Why, because you don't like bubbles?" She giggled.

"Yeah," I said as I shuffled into the kitchen. I snatched the sack with the outlet and trudged up the stairs. I'd learned that I could find out how to do just about any type of repair by watching DIY videos on the web. It had sort of become an addiction of mine. Mom made decent money selling real estate and all, but there was no need for her to pay for jobs I could take care of myself.

"You'll want to put some candles in there for Missy Moo," I told her. "I'll need to shut the lights out."

"Good idea." Mom gathered the battery-operated candles on the edge of her Jacuzzi tub. "Want me to get a flashlight for you?" she asked.

"Nope. Got my phone." I pried open the closet door at the top of the stairs and pulled out the colorful craft box we kept the tools in. I hollered at Mom to shut off breakers number five and six, and tore open the package of screws as I waited for the lights to go out.

Missy squealed with excitement once they did, and

declared from the other side of the wall that she'd want candlelight bubble baths forever and ever. I had bigger thoughts on my brain. Specifically the stuff Grandma and Grandpa had told me. Were boys really that clueless? Tell him what I needed. What I needed was an answer and that should most definitely go without saying. For crying out loud, I wasn't exactly asking him to be a mind reader. I wasn't the guess-what's-on-my-mind type of girl, was I?

TJ's ex-girlfriend, Tiffany, used to really mess with his head. *"Why didn't you do this for me?"* Or *"How come you didn't do that?"* She expected him to walk around with a crystal ball and predict her every possible need. According to him, anyway. But let's get real. This was a no brainer. You get asked to a dance, you answer someone. It's that simple. Anyone on the planet knows it.

So there. I'd rejected the idea that I was meant to heed to their well-intended, elderly advice in this regard. Jett was the one who was in the wrong here, and I didn't want to act like it was all right by replying to his text and inviting him to come over like he'd suggested. Especially if it meant he was just going to officially break things off.

Although, a very big part of me didn't believe that he would. Call it denial all you want, but I still kind of believed—somewhere deep in my heart—that Jett really had fallen for me. That he liked me even still.

Perhaps he'd just gotten distracted by Tasha at their assembly practice.

Maybe he just needed to realize that he could lose me too.

"Okay," I hollered. "You can switch the breaker back on."

"Switching . . ." my mom announced.

I heard splashing from the kid's bathroom. "I don't want them back on." The pitter patter that followed said she'd already figured out how to solve the problem herself by flipping down the switch. At once the lights in Mom's bathroom flashed back on, causing me to squint against the brightness.

I tugged open the oversized drawer in Mom's vanity, pulled out her hair dryer, and plugged it in. Mom walked in just as I flipped the switch. The small thing blasted into life with a hot hum.

"Thanks, hon," she said. "I don't know where I'd be without you."

I grinned, appreciating the kind words more than usual. I was needy tonight. "Night, Mom," I said after putting the hairdryer back in place. "Love you."

"Love you too, Harper boo."

I shuffled back into my room, my mind trying to work my way out of the mess I was in. I was so distracted by the thoughts in my brain that I almost missed the sight of the boy standing there. Blond scraggly hair, ripped jeans, and a leather jacket that smelled like smoke.

"TJ?" It came out in a squeak.

He hitched a thumb over his shoulder to point to my balcony door. "Sorry, thought this would be easier than trying to get past your mom."

I nodded for him to continue.

"I heard about Jett and Tasha, and I think I've got a plan."

I furrowed my brow as I scrutinized him. "A plan?" TJ wouldn't be caught dead at a school dance, so I couldn't imagine what kind of plan he might devise.

He tucked a thumb casually into his front pocket and tipped his head to one side. His eyes lit up with a new spark of mischief that said he'd probably earned more of that bad boy status than I'd given him credit for. "Let's go to the dance together."

CHAPTER FIFTEEN

I shrugged into my flannel shirt without an ounce of enthusiasm.

I'd counted at least half a dozen things I'd rather do than go to the dance with TJ tonight, one of which entailed scrubbing vomit from the dining room rug—a chore I'd acquired when Missy and Mom had the flu.

What had I been thinking when I agreed to this? Tonight I'd be stuck watching Tasha, my Mean Girl nemesis, petting the guy I'd been in love with my entire life. Just the idea triggered enough of my own flu-like symptoms to put me down for a week.

I fastened each small button with slow fingers, wondering if Jett would be wearing a flannel shirt too. Of *course* he would; it was 90's grunge, what else was there? TJ was stoked when he heard about the theme. He even called up Mrs. Parks, the school principal, to see if he and Grunge Town could play a live song or two during the dance. While Mrs. Parks declined his offer, insisting it was too late to make necessary arrangements, she told him she *would* make an exception to the rule about school dropouts coming to the dance, so long as he agreed to look into a course that would help him attain his GED.

That had to count for something, didn't it? Perhaps I'd play a role in TJ getting his life together after all. I let out a humorless laugh at the thought. Hadn't I given up on that idea yet?

The truth is, I was pretty sure I'd taken a bad situation and made it worse. The day after TJ asked me to go to the dance with him, I walked right up to Jett in the east hall and told him about it. I had spent the entire night rehearsing for it. I'd hopped out of bed extra early, spent extra time so I'd look as smoking hot as I could (for me, anyway) and fully expected to gain some sort of satisfaction from the act.

What I didn't expect was the expression that came over his face. It might have been the same look he'd give me if I reached out and slapped him. Or stabbed some massive hot poker through his chest.

To top it off, he didn't show up to first period. *Fine,* I'd told myself. *Let him have a turn being too distraught to sit through class.* It seemed terribly off balance though. Why have such a big reaction to something he'd caused in the first place? I was the one who should be angry.

I kept hearing Grams' and Gramps' advice in the back of my mind, practically begging me to speak up and communicate with the guy, but the woman scorned in me wouldn't allow it. Besides, Jett was the reason we were in this mess. Not only hadn't he replied to *my* invitation to the dance, he'd basically spit on it by telling Tasha yes when she'd asked in front of the entire school.

That was the last time I spoke to Jett. We hadn't called or texted one another since. Or said so much as a "hey" or "hi" in the hall. With new partners in first period, we sat on opposite sides of the room, which made it easy for me to escape before he had the chance to ignore me.

So it was official. Things between us—if they were ever real in the first place—were over now. At least I hadn't seen Tasha and Jett cuddling up to one another. That was a sight I did *not* want to see.

The blur of my reflection came back into focus as a knock sounded at my bedroom door. "TJ's here," Mom said as she stepped into my room. "He's downstairs looking at all of Missy's drawings."

She took a seat at the foot of my bed and looked me up and down. "What—did you raid my high school closet?" she asked with a laugh. "You look exactly like me when I was your age. Apart from the hair color." She swooped the blonde strands of her shoulder-length hair behind one ear.

I tried to picture her back in those days. She hadn't met my father until college. Her first frat party. It got the wheels in my mind turning. Thinking of the way fate had shoved TJ right back into my lap. After I'd tried very hard to let go and...let God, like Mom had suggested.

"Why did you start dating Dad?" I asked. It might not be the best time to have this conversation, but I really wanted to know what my role was regarding TJ. Whether

I ever wound up with Jett or not, I realized now that he was the type of guy I wanted.

"I liked him because he was funny and charming, and in some ways…well, he seemed to have just a very kind heart." She shrugged. "And because I sensed that he was good—really good—at heart, I figured I could fix him." She'd dropped her gaze to the floor, and for a moment, I saw a world of emotion rush through her.

She glanced back up to me, hints of moisture welling in her eyes, and gulped. "You're not in charge of fixing him, Harper. TJ might be just as kindhearted as your father, but that doesn't mean he'll become the man he could be. He *may*, he may not. That's all up to him."

I felt her words pierce the deepest part of me. The part that doubted I had the right to walk away. I heard what she'd said, and for the first time, I believed it. A great burst of emotion crashed over me, fuzzy and warm in my chest, assuring me that what she said was true.

I hadn't exactly given TJ up for the right reasons last time. It'd been more of a kneejerk reaction to what he'd done. But perhaps I needed this moment. Needed it so that I'd pursue the Jetts of the world, not the TJs.

Mom was off the bed and wrapping her arms around me in a blink. Shushing me gently as the sobs finally came. I wasn't going to have Jett. I was only now really letting myself realize that. Which meant I had two official goodbyes tearing at my chest. One with TJ, a guy I very much cared about. And Jett, the guy I'd started falling in love with. The one I could actually picture having a future with.

147

"I really wanted it to work with Jett Bryant," I admitted.

"It still might," she said as she rubbed my back. "It still might. Don't write him off just yet."

"Is anybody up there or what?" Missy hollered from downstairs. "TJ's been waiting for, like, a hundred years."

Mom and I chuckled, both wiping at tears. "Just one more minute," Mom hollered back. She brought a hand to my face and studied me for a blink. "You're so much wiser than I was at your age. Already you're seeing more clearly than I did back then." She sniffed, nodding. "Life doesn't come with any guarantees," she said, "but there's one thing I'll tell you for sure. You don't get very far in life by beating around the bush. If you're confused about something Jett's done...if it doesn't line up with the other things you know about him, then confront him. Give him the chance to explain himself, for crying out loud. You don't want to go through life haunted by *what ifs*, do you?"

I shook my head. "No. I've already got one of those where Jett's concerned," I admitted. "From clear back in the eighth grade."

"Oh yeah?"

I grinned. "I'll tell you about it later."

Mom rested a hand on my back, as we headed down the stairs. "Well, let's get a picture of you two. Can't live off selfies alone, can you?"

"I'm going to take so many selfies once I get my own phone," Missy promised as Mom positioned us by the door. I saw my mom in a new light then. A strong, independent woman who hadn't just gone out and found

CHEMISTRY OF A KISS

a replacement for Dad. And she'd had plenty of opportunity, I knew that much. She wasn't afraid to be alone. And I shouldn't be either.

I'd also decided there was a whole lot of wisdom in what she'd said. I couldn't just let this relationship go without confronting Jett. It wouldn't be tonight, of course. I wasn't about to make a scene, but someday soon I would show up at Jett's house and talk to him about what had happened. At least then, even if I was alone, I'd have some answers.

"Okee-doke," Mom said as she tucked her phone back into her pocket. "You guys better get going. Have a great time."

"Yeah, have a great time," Missy echoed.

"We will," I promised Missy before looking at my mom. "And thanks."

CHAPTER SIXTEEN

I thought more about what my mom said as we drove to the school. I thought it'd be best to at least get on the same page with TJ before we stepped inside the gymnasium.

"Hey," I said, stilling him at the doorway. Music from a band I didn't recognize echoed down the hallway. "I just want to go in and have a fun time tonight, okay?"

TJ nodded, but his face was already scrunching up in question.

"What I mean by that," I went to stipulate, but that's when I saw something my eyes could not pull away from: Tasha draping her long skinny arms over Jett's shoulders. She zeroed in on me like a hawk through the crowd and shot me a wicked grin.

"Never mind." I looped a hand around the nook in TJ's arm and yanked. "Let's dance." Wafts of perfume clashed with body odor as we weaved our way through the crowd, one dancing couple at a time. I stopped once we were roughly two yards from Jett and Tasha.

"Perfect," TJ growled under his breath. "We'll make them sorry they're not here with us." And suddenly he was pulling me against him and moving his hands very close to my rear end. It reminded me of the way he'd held Tasha at Burger Bar. Funny how he'd never even tried that while we dated. Funny, as in he knew better. Until now, that is.

Now it was all out war, which meant I wouldn't cause a fuss over it. As long as he didn't grab my butt completely.

The thought barely came to mind when TJ did exactly that. Both hands, all fingers and thumbs, solidly grabbed onto my rear end.

I squealed and shoved at his chest. "Don't," I warned, squaring a look at him. "*I'm* not a girl you can do that to, and you know it."

TJ had the nerve to roll his eyes, but he gave me a nod and stepped back up to me. He flattened his hands stiffly against my shoulder blades and gave them an awkward pat. "Like this?" he asked snidely. "Is this what you like?"

Well, at least TJ wasn't making it hard to put things to an end between us tonight. But that's when I remembered what was actually going on here. TJ hadn't asked me to come to this because he wanted me back; he wanted to come so that he could make Tasha jealous. Just like I'd wanted to make Jett sorry.

So what was this? A game of fake dating in reverse? It was ridiculous.

I hadn't let myself look back at Jett and Tasha yet, but

as we spun in place to the slow-paced song, coming to the spot where they'd be in view, I allowed my gaze to drift over them. Jett looked furious. Jaw tight, eyes narrowed, body rigid. It seemed he was glaring at the back of TJ's head. A glare that landed on me as we shifted our weight to the beat. And then we were facing opposite directions. Jett with his partner, me with mine.

I wondered if that meant that TJ and Tasha were facing one another now. As if answering my question, TJ moved in and started pressing kisses to my neck. I froze in place, my feet planting in one spot as I considered how far I wanted this game to go. It felt like I was selling my soul to the devil, and for what?

If witnessing TJ's groping session made Jett suddenly want me instead of Tasha, I'd be left to assume that he had more than an innocent relationship in mind. Which implied that there weren't a whole lot of good guys out there. Which suddenly made me want to just...cry and tear out of there all at the same time.

"Just let me grab your butt for a second so she can see," TJ pled. "She'll *freak*." At once he slid his hands down and grabbed, moving his sloppy kiss up the side of my neck.

I struggled in the constricted space, ready to swat him off me like a gargantuan fly, when someone pried him away from me. Before I could see who it was or what exactly they were doing, a fist slammed into TJ's face.

Adrenaline spiked through me so hard it hurt. I couldn't tear my eyes off the sight of TJ teetering on one foot, catching himself with the other, and then stumbling into the oblivious couple behind him.

I worked to drag my eyes off the scene, very aware of the crowd that was forming around us. I pressed my hand to my chest to catch my breath and spun to see who had started the fight. Heaven knew TJ had enough enemies to start a brawl here or half of the places around town, but I had not expected to see Jett standing so close. He was shaking out his fist and glaring at TJ.

"Jett!" Tasha screamed through the music as she caught up to him.

And so it *was* him. I gasped. *Jett* had landed a punch on TJ?

He shouldered his way around Tasha and lunged toward TJ, who was climbing back to his feet. "You like putting your hands on people? Let's see how you like it when I put my hands on you." He gripped hold of him by the shirt and forced him to his feet.

TJ swung, missed, but clocked Jett as he came in with another swing with his other fist.

Crap. TJ binged on wrestling matches. I had to get Jett out of this. Students rushed in to witness the fight, successfully pushing me back as I watched Jett ram an elbow into TJ's jaw. Maybe he liked watching those too.

A sharp, familiar-sounding whistle broke out as the music died. "Break it up, boys. Right now." Yep, that was Mr. Meadows' unmistakable whistle. I'd heard it a million times during play practice.

"Are you okay?" Another familiar voice came, this one from Ms. Tolken.

I tore my eyes off Jett as he smeared blood from his lip

to tell her that I was just fine. *Wait, maybe that's not who I heard.*

"Are you dizzy?" the woman asked. She looked different, but I couldn't exactly say why. Eye makeup maybe?

"Yeah," I said. "I mean, no. You look so pretty."

Ms. Tolken gave me a smile, then quickly erased it. "Let's go out into the hall and see what's going on here."

I nodded, propping myself onto my toes to see Mr. Meadows ushering TJ at one side, Jett at his other. "I don't know what happened," I said. The spin cycle had taken up residence in my chest, slamming ruthlessly against my ribcage as I tried catching my breath.

She stopped walking and turned back to look at me. "I know what happened," she said, a hint of pride coating her words. "You were championed by Jett Bryant."

"Championed?" I raised my brows.

Ms. Tolken held my gaze a moment more and nodded. "Let's go." With that, she led me toward the doorway, dodging the dispersing crowd as she went. I realized another change then; her polyester pants had been replaced by a pencil skirt, which showed off the woman's curvy legs. I *knew* she was secretly a hottie beneath all that junk she wore.

Mr. Meadows had both guys on the floor, shoved up against the wall, separated only by the closed utility closet door. Both had red welts on their faces, but I had to say, it looked like TJ took the worst of it. Which had me worrying about Jett and his scholarship and his position as captain of the basketball team.

That new knot of worry worked its way into my gut.

"Do you want to tell me what's going on here?" Mr. Meadows bellowed.

Ms. Tolken motioned for me to follow her to the adjacent wall. Jett shot me a lingering look before setting his gaze back on Meadows.

But TJ spoke up first. "Me and Harper were dancing..."

"Harper and *I*," Mr. Meadows corrected.

TJ's face scrunched up. "*What?*"

"That's the proper way to say it," Ms. Tolken said. "Continue."

TJ glanced at me for a blink, then shook his head. "We were dancing and suddenly Jett swoops in like Batman and sucker punches me in the face."

"It's not a sucker punch when you provoked it," Jett snapped, pulling away from the wall to glare at him.

"Hey, hey, hey." Mr. Meadows put his hands out. "Violence should be a last resort, Mr. Bryant. I'm sure you know that. In the years I've seen you play ball, you've practiced more self-control than I thought possible. You should have exercised some of that tonight. Coach isn't going to be happy."

"I was protecting her," Jett said, "and I'd do it again in a heartbeat." My heart, which hadn't even begun to recover, did a little flip.

Mr. Meadows spun to look at me over his shoulder.

"Did you need protecting?"

Now a full on gymnastic routine was happening inside my chest. I looked over at TJ. "I *did* tell him to take his hands off me," I said.

"It was just an act." TJ rolled his eyes. "We were trying to make our exes jealous."

"Oh, so *I'm* your ex now?" Jett asked.

I looked into his deep brown eyes, taken aback by the emotion I saw there. "I don't know what you are, Jett. All I know is that I asked you to the dance a week ago and you never answered. And *then* you say yes to Tasha in front of the entire school without ever acknowledging—"

Jett put his hand up to stop me. "Wait, did you say you asked me to the dance?"

"You asked him to the dance first?" TJ asked.

"I thought you knew that," I said.

"*Who?*" Both TJ and Jett looked at me, confusion crumpling their faces.

"Both of you," I said. "TJ, I thought you knew that I asked Jett and that he never answered me and that that's why I was so upset about him going with Tasha." I set my gaze on Jett next. "And you...why are you acting surprised? There's no way you didn't get what I left for you."

Jett's brow furrowed. "I didn't get anything from you, Harper."

We stayed like that while the music from the gym went from muted to loud. Someone had opened the door, I realized.

"It was a poster and it had pictures of us on it. There was other stuff too. Basketball balloons...you never saw those?"

Jett shook his head. "Seriously, Harper. I never saw it."

"*Wait* just a minute, Miss Martell," Ms. Tolken said.

I looked over my shoulder in time to see Tasha sneaking back into the gym. She stopped in her tracks, shoulders dropping, and let the door swing to a close. "I don't know anything about it," Tasha said with wide, innocent eyes. "If you ask me, any good wind could come along and sweep that stuff right off his porch."

I fought back an eye-roll. "Yeah, right."

"Wait," Jett said. "How did *you* know it was on my porch?" His eyes narrowed in a hard glare.

Tasha cinched the flannel tighter around her waist and squirmed in place. "Everyone knows you ask people by leaving candy and stuff on the porch."

"I never said I left candy either," I snapped.

"I can't believe you asked me, Harper," Jett said. "I was trying to hint to you that whole time. I knew I'd have to say yes to the first girl who asked and I wanted that to be you."

I hurried over to him and got onto the floor at his side. "I thought you were just teasing me. Until you said yes to Tasha, which really threw me off…"

"No wonder." Jett cupped a gentle hand to my face. He came in, brushed his bruised lips over mine. "I'm so sorry," he said.

I shook my head. *"I'm* sorry that I didn't just mention it."

"Okay, okay," Mr. Meadows barked, putting his arms up once more. "Let's get back on track here." He pointed a finger at Jett. "Coach isn't going to be happy when he hears about this." He moved the pointed finger to TJ. "And you—I could have Sheriff Lang here in two seconds flat."

"Can't we just let everyone say that they're sorry and let it drop?" I asked, hurrying to my feet. I approached Meadows and looked him in the face. "This really wouldn't have happened if it wasn't for the whole misunderstanding." I shot Tasha a look, but she was admiring her bright green fingernails.

"I think we're past that point—" Mr. Meadows started to say, but Ms. Tolken stepped in and put a hand on his shoulder.

"Don't you think that…" Her lashes fluttered, making me realize she'd tugged off her glasses. I glanced down to see she held them behind her back. Mr. Meadows' face flushed red.

"If everyone is willing to drop it, there's no sense in getting these kids—and they *are* usually very good kids— into trouble."

I couldn't believe my ears. Or my eyes. This was a completely different woman than the one in polyester. TJ had called Jett Batman, which wasn't far off if you asked me, but perhaps we had our very own Catwoman here at Sweet Water High as well.

"Well," Mr. Meadows said with a one-shoulder shrug. He swiped a hand through his wavy hair, nodded, and turned his gaze back to Jett and TJ. "*Are* you guys willing to drop all of this?"

TJ tipped his head. "Tasha," he said. "Why did you do that? You told me that it was Coach's idea for you to ask Jett since he didn't have a date. What—you just wanted *him* all along?"

Tasha puffed out a loud breath and tipped her head

back. "Can we just get out of here?" She looked over at me. It was the first time I'd seen her look...embarrassed. She set her gaze back on TJ. "Look, I'm sorry. I'll tell you more later. Let's just go."

TJ shook his head. "I'm willing to let this drop. I'm sorry for grabbing your butt, Harper," he said, looking at me like a repentant child. "I know you're not that kind of girl and I shouldn't have done it."

Sure, it sounded a little rehearsed, but something told me that TJ was, in fact, sorry.

"I just really wanted to make Tasha regret asking Jett," he continued. "I didn't know that Harper had asked him. And I definitely didn't know Tasha made it look like you didn't by doing...whatever she did."

Tasha leaned heavily on one hip and sighed.

Meadows and Tolken set their eyes on me expectantly.

"Harper?" Ms. Tolken prompted.

"I accept your apology," I said.

"Jett?" Meadows said.

Jett looked between TJ and me, then turned back to Mr. Meadows. "I'm good if she's good," he said. "As long as he keeps his hands off her from here on out," he added under his breath.

Mr. Meadows nodded to Ms. Tolken. "We can't exactly keep this between us since half the school witnessed it, but we *can* let Principal Parks know that you and I took care of the matter and saw fit to let things drop."

A massive weight lifted from my shoulders. Jett had a lot riding on his basketball career, and I was grateful that this wouldn't put that at risk. I wanted to give both Mr.

Meadows and Ms. Tolken a big giant hug, but I settled for a "thank you so much!" instead. I thanked TJ too, and he headed out and into the parking lot alone.

Tasha, also flying solo now, scurried back into the gym, but not before mumbling something to Jett about finding his own ride home.

"We'll let you two talk," Ms. Tolken said once the four of us were left in the hall. She grabbed Mr. Meadows' elbow, and together, the two chaperones returned to the party.

"Was she your ride?" I asked.

Jett nodded.

"We can catch a ride with Bailey and Summer," I said with a laugh.

Jett shuffled closer, resting his head in the nook between my shoulder and neck. "I feel so bad for not answering you."

I clenched my eyes shut, remembering the time I'd almost texted him about it. "It's not your fault. I'm the one who should've at least asked you about it."

Jett took hold of my hand, brought it to his lips, and pressed a gentle, lingering kiss to my palm. My body went limp, every limb softening like overcooked noodles. All of the feels and thrills we'd read about sparked into action as he moved along my wrist in a slow rhythm.

He glanced up at me then, keeping ahold of my wrist, and wrapped his other hand solidly around my hip where he gave me a squeeze.

Goosebumps rippled over my skin.

"Harper Tisdale," he said. "Just so you know, I really *really* like you."

"I really *really* like you too," I said as a giggle snuck out.

"I'd love it if you'd be my girlfriend. Will you?"

I bit my lip and grinned. "Yes."

And there was that gorgeous dimple. *"Yes,"* he said with a fist pump. He moved his hand back to my hip then, and his gaze dropped to my mouth.

I couldn't help but look at his yummy lips in return as all those sensors started into action once more. It was part of our ceremony. The ritual. A thing I'd come to call the chemistry of a kiss.

He leaned down and pressed his lips to mine in a full, dreamy exchange that had me grasping onto his shoulders as a sigh sounded in my throat.

Best. Kisses. Ever.

"Let's go dance," he mumbled against my lips.

"Sounds good to me."

Jett led me into the gym just as a Pearl Jam song kicked on. One of my favorites. We found Bailey and Summer's group soon enough, and joined in on the fun, playing air guitar one moment, while swaying to the rhythm the next.

Kissing Jett might be one of my favorite things, but I was glad we knew how to have fun hanging out together as well. As a new song picked up, Emmy came around with her camera and had us pose for a pic. Jett hoisted me right off the ground and cradled me for the pose. The other guys in the group followed suit as the girls squealed, creating what was sure to be a fun shot.

"Awesome," Emmy said as her boyfriend Ky wrapped

his arm around her. Looked like it was time to pass the camera on. I hoped someone would be getting pictures of those two together as well.

I glanced around the gym, eyeing all the couples that had gotten together over the last few months. A dose of warmth and gratitude filled my heart. Senior year was off to an incredible start, and I couldn't wait to see what the rest of the year might bring.

Not to mention the rest of the evening.

Tonight was sure to include a deeper conversation about the last few days, which was good. I looked forward to being more open with Jett, and taking my brilliant grandparents' advice as best I could. Of course, I assumed the evening would end with another incredible kiss. The very idea made goosebumps race up my arms while my heart did a little dance of its own.

Our assignment might be over, but Jett was my boyfriend now, which meant we'd get to study the topic a whole lot more.

That was definitely something to look forward to.

"Is the ham ready?" Missy spun her way over to the counter, gracefully picked up the basket of rolls, and tiptoed her way to the dining room table.

"Almost," Mom said as she pried open the oven. "Come look at the glaze. It's getting brown and bubbly."

I abandoned the napkin folding long enough to join Missy and Mom at the oven. The fact that we were actually having so many normal foods today made this Christmas Eve dinner extra special. Sure, Mom spent a couple hundred dollars to get a ham and glaze that met her strict standards, and the mixed veggies and fruit salad were up to those standards too, but Mom threw caution to the wind by letting me pick out fresh bakery rolls at the market. *Go Mom!*

Better yet, Mom wasn't the one in charge of the cheesy potatoes this year. One of our special guests was bringing them. A guest who'd learned from the woman who usually baked those cheesy potatoes for every funeral, sick home, or special event at Sweet Water Worship. That's right. Jett and his dad were coming over for dinner.

It'd been more of a last minute thing. Ava and Ivy had flown out to spend time with their grandmother for the first half of winter break. There hadn't been any change in his parents' situation, as far as Jett knew, but he was hopeful. Anyway, the twins planned to travel back here with Cathy so the family could spend Christmastime together, which seemed like a good sign. Sadly, their flight had been delayed, and when Mom heard about it, she extended the offer and they said yes. *Bam!*

Missy and I helped Mom with the last minute preparations before the guests arrived. Christmas songs played softly from the speakers I'd installed last week. Potted chrysanthemums were placed on each side table, their scarlet petals and green leaves adding the perfect Christmas color splash. I couldn't help but admire the beautiful gold ring Jett had bought me last week. This one had a snowflake to represent our first winter as a couple.

Grams and Gramps came first, and then my incredibly handsome boyfriend and his dad. Dating the pastor's son turned out not to be *too* awkward since Pastor Bryant was such a cool guy. Even cooler, I decided, when I saw that he brought a gorgeous cream pie that was sure to taste as good as it looked since he, unlike Mom, bought normal stuff.

Dinner was perfect. Incredible food, delicious drinks in fancy glasses—courtesy of Grams and her sparkling cider "for the kids"—and a whole lot of heartfelt laughter.

Most of that was brought on by Gramps and his stories of Christmas past. Some when he was young, a few from when he and Grams were dating, and a touching one about my mom when she was a little girl. I hadn't heard it before, but she'd snuck over to the neighbor's Christmas morning with her Christmas cash—twenty dollars, which was a lot for a seven-year-old—and slipped it into their mailbox. Apparently, her friend's father had been laid off.

The Christmas spirit came alive with that story, and also while we took turns reading the Christmas story out of the gospels beside the fireplace. Jett and I offered to clean up while the rest of the group lounged in the living room, watching Missy spin around to the carols.

I bumped Jett's elbow with mine as we stood side-by-side at the sink. "Merry Christmas," I said.

Jett dipped a finger into the mounding bubbles and dabbed it onto my nose with a grin. "Merry Christmas to you."

My hands deep in the suds, I rubbed the tiny bubbles with my sleeve. "Did you see where I put the mistletoe?" I asked while handing over a plate.

Jett dunked it in the rinse, rubbing at the surface before placing it in the rack. "Nope," he said. "But I've been looking for it, trust that."

I glanced over my shoulder to see the group was enthralled by Missy's invisible tightrope act. The girl knew how to entertain, that was sure. "Come here," I said, snatching a hand towel to dry my hands. Jett used it next, then followed me over to the pantry. He looked up at the bare wall above the doorframe, but I shook my head and pulled open the door.

He stepped inside and tipped his head back. A wide grin came over his face. "Nice."

I lifted a brow. "Right? I'm thinking of leaving it there year-round."

"That's a good idea." He snatched me by the hand and yanked me inside with him. Suddenly it got dark, which told me he'd pulled the door closed behind me. His hands cupped my hips as he placed a series of soft, tempting kisses over my cheek.

"You know that thing I said in class about romantic chemistry? That I didn't think it was a real thing?"

"Umm hmm." He moved to a spot very close to my earlobe, causing a rush of euphoria to pour over me. "I remember," he assured, his hot breath teasing my skin.

"Well, I lied."

Jett pulled back. "Does that mean you *don't* have...what did you specify back then...love and respect for me?"

I shook my head. "Nope. We just happen to have all three."

Jett leaned in and pressed his lips to mine in a heavenly, lingering kiss, proving that I would never grow immune to the effect he had on me. "You're right," he mumbled, kissing me again. And then once more—a wonderful, mind-tingling kiss.

A moment later he pushed the door open and took hold of my hands. "We better finish these dishes so we can break out the pie. I saw you eying that thing."

I laughed. "Yeah, but did you see me graze the top with a spoon and take a taste?"

He chuckled. "You wouldn't do that."

"I was tempted," I said.

As we made our way back to the sink, I thought back on the other topic Ms. Tolken brought up that day. The one about being able to make people change. I no longer believed I *could* force someone to change. I did, however, believe that it was important to speak up, as Gramps suggested. Jett and I were putting that in practice quite a bit, and it had brought us closer already.

Time would only tell if the future would bring what we hoped it might, but so far, with the two of us going to the same school, and plans of carpooling and summer vacations already in the works, we were off to a very good start. And for a season as wonderful and promising as Christmastime was, I couldn't think of a better gift.

FREE BOOK

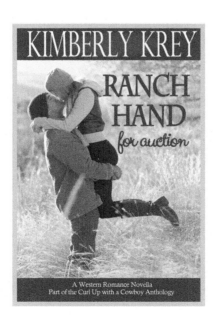

Subscribe to my newsletter and receive my novella, Ranch Hand for Auction, FREE as a thank you gift!

ABOUT THE AUTHOR

Writing Romance That's Clean Without Losing the Steam!

Award-winning author Kimberly Krey has always been a fan of good, clean romance, so she decided to specialize in writing 'Romance That's Clean without Losing the Steam'. She's a fervent lover of God, family, and cheese platters, as well as the ultimate hater of laundry. Follow her on any of the sites below for updates on new releases and or giveaways.

facebook.com/kimberlykreyauthor

twitter.com/KimberlyKrey

instagram.com/romance_is_write

bookbub.com/profile/kimberly-krey

ALSO BY KIMBERLY KREY

Unlikely Cowgirl Series

Once Hitched Twice Shy

How to Catch a Cowboy in 10 Days

This Cowboy's a Keeper

Country Brides & Cowboy Boots ~ Cobble Creek Romance

The Sheriff's Bride

The Lumberjack's Bride

The Snapshot Bride

The Sweet Montana Bride Series

Reese's Cowboy Kiss

Jade's Cowboy Crush

Cassie's Cowboy Crave

Second Chances Series

Rough Edges

Mending Herats

Fresh Starts

Beach Romance

Catching Waves: A Sweet Beach Romance (The Royal Palm
Resort Book 2)

Made in the USA
Coppell, TX
07 December 2020

43601289R00104